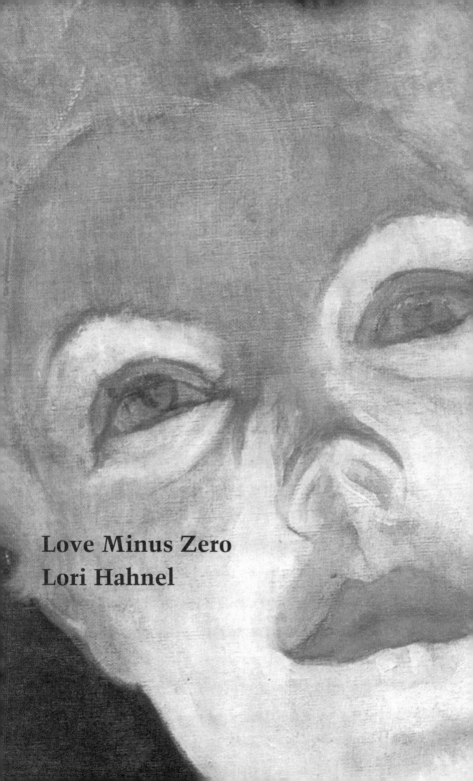

Love Minus Zero
Lori Hahnel

Copyright © 2008 by Lori Hahnel

The publishers acknowledge the support of the Canada Council for the Arts, the Ontario Arts Council, the Government of Ontario through the Ontario Media Development Corporation and the Government of Canada through the Book Publishing Industry Development Program for their publishing activities.

I would like to thank my dear friends and fellow writers Diane Girard, for her careful reading of this material, her encouragement and camaraderie; and Rona Altrows, for her trusty editorial eye and ear, for offering a shoulder and for just being a mensch. Thank you to the hardworking staff at Calgary Public Library for everything. Thanks to Mary Welin and Catherine Cartmill for helping me to remember. I am grateful to Mark Jarman for his vision and his caring edit, and to Oberon Press for making this book happen. Last but not least, heartfelt thanks to Bruce, Nick and Dan for your love, support and patience.

ISBN 978 0 7780 1330 3 (hardcover)
ISBN 978 0 7780 1331 0 (softcover)

Cover art by Henri de Toulouse-Lautrec
Edited by Mark Anthony Jarman
Book design by Michael Macklem

Printed in Canada

PUBLISHED IN CANADA BY OBERON PRESS

 Canada Council   Conseil des Arts
for the Arts   du Canada

 ONTARIO ARTS COUNCIL
CONSEIL DES ARTS DE L'ONTARIO

To Bruce

1. Saturday, 19 August 2006

Niall's still a good dancer. I wonder if he's still an asshole? I guess I should give him a chance. I mean, I haven't seen him in over twenty years, not since that night at The National. And people change, or at least you hope they do. I know I have. He looks different, all right. He's put on some weight and there's something going on with his hair. I mean, most men his age lose hair, but he seems to be gaining it. It's still blond and all over the place. Dancing with him again is weird, and dancing with him at Jude's wedding, no less— that's really weird. Of course, we're not dancing close or anything, and the song is The Buzzcocks' *Ever Fallen in Love (With Someone You Shouldn't Have Fallen in Love With)?* Ha.

But it is kind of a weird wedding. There's the bride, dancing away in her wedding mosh pit with the other bride, and both brides look beautiful. And having it at the Hillhurst-Sunnyside Community Hall was a stroke of genius. That's Jude's sense of humour for you. The place is exactly the same, which just accentuates how we're all not. One thing that's missing is the blue cloud of cigarette smoke that used to float around at these things. Now the few smokers left (and I'm no longer among them) have to go outside. People are drinking for sure, but nobody's going apeshit like we used to. Of course, that's probably precisely why none of us can drink much anymore. And we're just old, face it. I mean, when Joe Strummer died of a heart attack I felt really old. And that's already getting to be a long time ago. God.

Funny, I always said I never wanted to marry. Niall didn't believe me. I guess he was right not to believe me, because I did end up getting married, although not to him. Now here we both are at this wedding, and I don't know what I feel for him anymore at all. I thought at first maybe it was because we look different, so much more, er, mature. But it's more than that. It feels like we're different people, like we're strangers. Strange. It's been so long. I couldn't have even imagined being this old in those days. Thirty was about as far ahead as I could see into the future then, and even thirty seemed like a million years away.

Another thing that's missing is Maggie. It's times like this with the old crowd that I miss her most. Not that Jude would have invited her; they never had much use for each other. But she came to gigs at this hall how many times? How many times just to see us play? She even met Derek here. Wow. Man, that was a long time ago. When people die, they leave little things. I have a silver ring Maggie gave me a long time ago, and for years it just sat in a drawer. But since the accident, when she drove us through a railing on the Langevin Bridge, I wear it all the time. I feel sad, guilty sometimes when I look at it. I guess I'm too sentimental to stop wearing it, though.

Yes, Niall and I have changed. But it's good to see his smile's still the same. I just hope it doesn't have the same effect on me as it used to.

2. Friday, 17 October 1980

The metal v-shaped sign mounted on the brick wall over the doorway of The National Hotel said "Tavern Entrance" on either side. You went up a step to the heavy painted metal doors with little mesh-reinforced windows in them. Katya usually stood around these doors when we came in weekend nights to see the bands. Of course, she was there all the other nights of the week, too. She wasn't that much older than us, not even two years older than her sister Magdalena, whom we all called Maggie, and she didn't look very different from us. Her hair wasn't even as blond as mine, although hers was natural. Her skirts were maybe a little shorter, maybe she wore a little more eyeliner. But something on her face, in her eyes, told you she wasn't here to listen to music and drink National Hotel draft like the rest of us. She was working. That Friday night I remember she looked tired, like she hadn't been eating right or something.

I put my amp down for a second. "How are you?" I asked.

"Okay, Kate. I'm okay." She smiled like it was a ridiculous question, shook her head a little, held the door open for me. "Break a leg, tonight, eh?"

"I will. Come in and see us. We're on first."

"Yeah, I'll try to."

The place was pretty empty so far, just a sea of round red formica tables and orange vinyl-and-chrome chairs that went with the orange, gold and brown splotch pattern carpet. Maggie, who'd stormed past Katya, had a table right up at the front near the stage. She fussed with her long, dark hair in her compact mirror, stowed her purse under the table and settled in her chair, wouldn't look at me.

"What do you always have to go and talk to her for?" she finally asked.

"I guess I can if I want to. Why don't you talk to her? She's your sister."

"Not anymore, she's not."

We'd talked about Katya many times before and Maggie just refused to acknowledge her. I took my stuff up to the stage and left Maggie to stew by herself. Stage fright had me in its grip for the first of many times. My guitar case slipped in my cold, clammy hands, I felt my jaw set. I probably looked like I was going to a funeral or something. Clare taped our set list onto the floor of the stage among the cables and wires that snaked around our feet.

Three bands were on the roster that night: Misclairol, Emergency Exit and Extreme Unction. I was all nerves, didn't know what I was doing, wandered back and forth in a haze of anxiety. *This is ridiculous. What are we doing here? We can't play. Besides, Wendy isn't even here yet.*

But then there she was. It figured that the one time I'd hoped she'd show up late, or not at all, that she'd arrive in plenty of time. Wendy Wilson was our new drummer, the only one of us who wasn't underage, though no-one at The National ever said anything about that. We'd ambushed her from another band. Finding a female drummer was no easy task and when we heard of a metal band, Concubine, with a female drummer, we had to see them. We approached Wendy

7

after their set was over and she jumped at the chance to quit. She was a year older than me, and she listened to Elvis Presley, Joy Division and Led Zeppelin. She tolerated more than enjoyed most of the material we did, but she seemed happy enough. She was small and wore her long, red hair in a Farrah feather, and had a fondness for fringed clothing.

When the time came for our sound check we plugged in our guitars. Wendy started to get her bearings behind Extreme Unction's drums. The stage looked so much bigger when you stood on it. The lights were bright and hot, cords and cables tangled everywhere. I knew Clare was nervous, too. She looked like a pale, nervous Chrissie Hynde. And she seemed so far away. What if I had to ask her something, like what my name was or how to play a B flat chord? We tuned up, ran through a number. I felt like someone else was playing my guitar, and who was that singing? Through the monitors, our voices were strangers. We'd never heard ourselves so loud before. Every mistake would be magnified, I thought, as my stomach churned. Could the sounds we made fill up the place the way the other bands' did? Did we want them to?

When we finished, the sound man told us to leave our guitars on the stage, since we were up first. I felt lightheaded. *What could they do if I took off right now? Does Barb know the words to my songs? They could do it.* But I knew I couldn't really leave, despite the pleading and screaming of every cell in my body. I could go and throw up, though.

Vomiting provided me with some small relief. Then our bass player Barb came into the ladies' room. She was a tall girl with sea-green eyes and long, dark brown hair (by our next gig to become short, jet-black hair). She went to St. Vitus, and Clare and I went to St. Dymphna, but we'd met in the summer at a gig at Hillhurst-Sunnyside.

She looked at our reflections in the mirror as I reapplied my lipstick with a shaking hand. "Well," she said. "You look like fucking hell."

"Thanks, Barb. I feel like fucking hell."

"Did you just get sick?"

"I did. I have been on and off all day. Aren't you nervous?"

"Sure, I'm nervous. But it's not a firing squad, you know.

They're just a bunch of punk rockers. Who cares what they think? And anyway, we'll be great. I mean, look how fine we look. Couple of busty babes like us, wouldn't matter what we did. They're going to love us."

"I don't know. I think I look fat in this shirt."

"Fat? Not a chance. What you look is built, girl."

I never understood Barb's self-assurance. Where I saw fat, she saw built. How amazing to be like that, to have this deep well of confidence. Or appearing to, anyway. "Personally, I hope we'll sound okay. I hope we don't fuck up supremely. I don't particularly want breasts to be the focus here."

"Lighten up. Look at it this way: if we're good, the breast thing is just icing. And if we're bad, the breasts are a distraction. We can't lose either way."

I winced. "And if we really suck, we can always tear our shirts off."

She clapped my back as we left the washroom. "Now you've got it! What you need is a drink."

"Ladies, ladies," said Dave Graham, Niall's older brother. Dave and Niall looked something alike, both tall and spare, but Dave was darker and had blue eyes. Extreme Unction had finished their sound check and he drank something from a convenience store Slush cup that I guessed wasn't all Slush. "Haven't you heard that the band that stays straight together plays great together?"

Barb rolled her eyes. "I didn't mean she should get shit-faced, Dave. Don't be such a granny. She needs something to calm her down. She's about ready to lose it."

He looked at me, shook his head. "You know, you don't look so good. Maybe you need some fresh air."

"Great. Not only can I not play guitar, I look like shit, too. What am I doing here?"

"Whoa, whoa. Did I say that? You'll be fine after some air. And you look great. Come on out here for a minute."

A cold wind blew through the shady alley behind The National. My white knuckles gripped the stair rail. I formed a plan to hang on all night, until everyone else had left. Dave touched the back of my hand, looked surprised to find it cold. "Are you okay?"

9

"No, I'm not okay. I think I'm going to die. This is insane. We are not ready for this. We've got one set made up of covers and two three-chord originals, and that's it."

"And what do you think everybody else will play? I think Barb is right. You *do* need a drink," he said, and offered me the end of his rum-laced Slush. "Listen, this is your first time out. You'll be fine. Your sound check went great. Besides, you can't back out now. You're on in fifteen minutes."

I finished the drink and followed him back inside, felt better. Especially after the swig of rye someone offered me. Of course he was right. This was not a huge deal. Then again, it was easy for him to be confident, with his kind of talent. He could have played the keyboard stuff he did for Extreme Unction in his sleep. Once as I walked by the music-room at school I heard this amazing piano music, Bach, I think. Dave was in there alone and I sat down and listened to him for about twenty minutes before I had to leave for work. He blew me away. I'd never heard anybody play like that before. He didn't even notice me. He was completely absorbed, and I thought about how that's such a great place to be. Yeah, if I could play like that I wouldn't be worried, either.

Then it was time. We got onto the stage, picked up our guitars, turned them on. My voice rose up from somewhere deep inside. To me, it sounded high-pitched, far-off, like someone else. Someone I didn't know.

"Good evening. We're Misclairol."

Somehow, we got through it. Our set consisted of fifteen songs, my favourites being The Partridge Family's *I Think I Love You* and The Clash's *Janie Jones.* After the first three songs, we relaxed, even got to enjoy it in a masochistic kind of way. We made mistakes, there was discord, forgotten lyrics. I couldn't tell if Wendy was speeding up and slowing down all the time, or if it was the rest of us. But we had a cheering section, and seeing some familiar faces up front in the crowd helped. Sometimes it seemed like that's what these things were all about: to see which band had more friends. Nervousness compressed our 45 minute set to 35. We must sound like The Dickies, I thought as I milled out the chords as fast as Wendy demanded. The heat from the stage lights made sweat stream from our faces and bodies, but I soon discovered the lights were my friends, too. If I stood in a certain spot they blinded me, and once I figured that out I stayed rooted in place.

Finally, we finished. They clapped. Was this an encore? Then again, how many bands *didn't* get asked for encores? We churned out another three-chord Clash tune and then we were done, really this time. Later there would be arguments about who sped up all the time (Wendy), who had too much to drink (Kate), who sang off-key (Clare) and who paid more attention to the men in the audience than to the music (Barb). Still, it was over. Now we could relax.

"That was a lot of fun," I admitted, when we got off the stage. People came up and congratulated us. Most of them I knew, some of them I didn't. One girl, a tall redhead in a fuchsia mini-dress, looked familiar but I couldn't place her.

"My name's Judith Morrison. I go to St. Dymphna, too," she explained.

"That's where I've seen you. Do you go to any of the other shows?"

"This is the first one I've been to. Besides when XXX played at school that time."

"No way. You were there?"

"Yeah. And I wasn't even one of the people throwing stuff. Crazy, wasn't it?"

"It was insane."

"Anyway, I just wanted to tell you I enjoyed you guys tonight. Will you play again soon?"

"I don't know. I hope so. Gonna stick around for the other bands?"

"I don't think I can. Maybe I'll see you on Monday, though."

"Sure. Nice to meet you."

I appreciated all the attention in a way, but right then I just wanted to sit down and enjoy a quiet cigarette. I never pictured myself as a smoker, but once I tried it, it seemed as natural as breathing. Then Niall came over to our table, got down on his knees and kissed my hand.

"You girls did a great job. Congratulations." A stage light

backlit his blond hair. I longed to tousle it, didn't dare. I wondered what the stubble on his chin felt like. Scratchy, I guessed. I swallowed. So much for relaxing. "Thanks, Niall. I'm just glad it's over."

"Pretty scary the first time, isn't it? So where's the rest of Misclairol? I'd hoped to congratulate all of you."

"Well, Clare's off with her new boyfriend, Mikhail. You know, he drums for Schadenfreude. Wendy has left the building. Not her crowd, you know. And Barb is over chatting up some guy."

"I guess I'll have to kiss you again, then. Stand up," he said.

I did. He put his arms around me and crushed me up against his body as his hands slid to the small of my back. He lowered his head, lips almost brushed mine. Then he seemed to change his mind, and instead kissed behind my ear. "Good work," he whispered. Then he let go and walked over to get a beer, smiled over his shoulder at me. *Oh, God, don't do things like that. You have no idea. Do you?*

3. Saturday, 6 December 1980

The other bar the punk bands played at was in The Calgarian Hotel, a cozy little spot in the East End. The night The Sisters of Mercy, Niall's new band, opened for Safety Last from Edmonton, the place was packed. The Calgarian made The National look swanky. I don't know what it was. The tough-looking hookers who hung around outside, the scary-looking career drinkers who hung out in the front end of the bar? Maybe it was the beer absorbers. Soggy, almost worn-out red terry-towel beer absorbers covered the tables. If you forgot yourself and leaned on the table, you got soaked with draft. The carpet was worn down to the floor in many places and it was almost impossible to tell what colour it might have been originally. Heavy cardboard cutouts of horseshoes and cowboy hats decorated the tiny dance floor and stage areas.

They looked like they'd always been there and were probably still there when the hotel burned down six years later. The combined smells of cheap draft, smoke, cooking grease, dust, disinfectant, sweat, urine and vomit permeated the place, and finished with an ominous hint of sweetness. Clare, Barb and I sat near the dance floor, and Judith joined us for the first time. She didn't seem sure what to make of the place.

"You're supposed to order two of those glasses of draft at once?" she asked.

"Well, I guess you don't have to. You could just order one. But they're small, and the service is slow. Everybody just orders two."

Judith shrugged. "You look great, by the way, I wanted to tell you. That dress is beautiful." I wore a fitted dark blue and green brocade dress with rhinestone buttons down the front.

"Thanks. I like it, too."

"Did you get that at The Salvation Army?"

"Of course."

Finally the band got up on the stage. The Sisters were a three-piece. John Petersen played bass and reminded me of Iggy Pop. He had black hair, intense green eyes and a lean, wiry body. Niall handled vocals and guitar. A longhair called Hammerhead played drums. Nobody knew his real name, the story went. They played energetic, fast, power-chord stuff: Sham 69, Damned and Buzzcocks covers, some originals. The crowd went nuts, and seemed to be having almost as much fun as The Sisters.

I noticed a small woman approach the stage after their set. I thought she must be almost as old as my mother, 35 or so, anyway. She wore a red spandex jumpsuit, her hair was a dull orange frizz. She threw her arms around Niall's neck and whispered in his ear. He looked red-faced momentarily, then walked away. Just an insane fan, I guessed as my jaw and shoulders relaxed again.

In fact, he seemed to want to be with me. We danced together through Safety Last's first set, he had his arm around my shoulders through the first set break. He was getting drunk fast, though. I knew he'd been nervous before they played, since it was their first time out, so I could see how easy it would be to let loose afterwards. After all, that first time is scary as I well knew.

After a while, he took my chin in his hand and tilted my face up to his. My heart raced like a hamster's, a million tiny beats a minute. I tried to think what to say. His eyes scanned my face, looked for something. I wasn't sure I wanted to know what, funnily. Maybe he knew what I was thinking, because he dropped his hand.

"Did I tell you that's a great dress?"

"No. I mean, thanks."

"Want to come outside and smoke a joint with me?"

"Okay," I said and remembered to breathe, unsure whether I felt disappointed or relieved.

We got our jackets and went out the back door into the alley. Perfect place to smoke. The city lights tinted the dark clouds pink, the cold winter downtown smell of car exhaust hung in the air along with the clouds of our breath and our smoke. Soon Dave came looking for his brother and decided to join us in a wee hoot. Cold as it was, we stood and talked and laughed in the alley for what seemed like a long time. Then a woman in a faux leopard coat stumbled out the bar's back door, looked disoriented until her eyes adjusted to the dark and she spotted Niall.

"There you are!" She had a drink in one hand and a cigarette in the other. She threw her arms around Niall, spilled some of her rye and seven on his black leather jacket, and kissed him. This was the woman from before I realized, and everything suddenly seemed to move in slow motion. "Our cab's out front," she purred.

"Um, okay," Niall fumbled. He looked embarrassed. But not too embarrassed to follow her. "I'll see you guys later. I guess I won't need a ride home, Dave," he said, and looked back over his shoulder.

I stood frozen in place, watched snowflakes fall in the space where Niall had stood.

Dave looked disgusted. "I don't know what he's thinking. That woman's sucking 40."

"Who is that?"

"I think her name's Marianne. Haven't you seen her before?

She always hangs around and looks for boys to take home. I mean, she's got to be twice his age. And I thought there might be something starting up between you two," he said. I turned away from him.

"What's the matter?" he asked.

"Nothing. I was just starting to think the same thing," I said, ashamed of the stupid, awkward tears rolling down my face.

"Oh, shit. Really?" He put his arm around me. "I'm sorry. I'm sorry he's such an asshole. Let me give you a ride home."

I nodded, and he led me through the blurry, black, icy parking-lot to his car.

Even though Dave got me home before midnight I didn't sleep until very late that night. I was tired, but wired: all the evening's strange events ran through my head over and over and I could not make sense of them. I got up around eleven the next morning and poked around the kitchen for some coffee. The TV blared from the living-room and a bottle of rye and an empty ice cube tray stood on the counter. Was Carmen asleep? If she was I'd be able slip off to Clare's for practice. I peeked out and saw her dozing on the couch. So far, so good. Maybe I could grab an undisturbed bite before I went out.

I opened a cupboard slowly, quietly, found bread and a jar of peanut butter, set them on the counter gently so as to make no noise. Pulled out the cutlery drawer slowly so it wouldn't squeak and got a knife. Got a glass, let the water trickle into it. Found a saucer for my sandwich and set it down noiselessly on the counter. I was the master of doing things quietly from a lot of practice. You never knew what kind of mood Carmen would be in if you woke her up (she always insisted I call her 'Carmen', never 'Mom' or 'Mommy'). Sometimes she was fine, genial, even. Other times she was pure hostility undercut with embarrassment. So I was good at doing things quietly. Just like I was good at disappearing into the wallpaper when necessary.

Halfway through my sandwich the phone rang. "Damn," I exhaled, and sprang to answer it. Carmen was a light sleeper unless she was passed out.

"Hello," I whispered. "No. No. You've got the wrong number."

I replaced the phone in its cradle and listened for a few moments. Sure enough, I heard her stir, then walk toward the kitchen. *Fuck. Fucking idiot wrong goddam number.*

"Kate, are you home?"

"In the kitchen."

She joined me at the kitchen table, drink in hand. Her frizzy blond hair was a tangle, makeup smeared. "Just resting my eyes for a few minutes," she explained and propped her puffy face in her hands. "How long have you been here?"

"I just got up. I didn't want to bother you."

She dug around in the pockets of the blue housecoat wrapped around her bony body. The blue accented the knotty veins in her scrawny arms, all of them visible beneath the thin, transparent skin. Sometimes the way she looked scared me. I always thought that if she banged herself on something, she'd just bleed to death right on the spot. Then again, she was 37. I supposed people just dropped dead all the time at that age. Natural causes, it would say in the paper.

"You were out at that Calgarian place again last night, weren't you?"

"Yeah."

"You're underage. Don't they even check for ID?"

"Sometimes. They've never asked me, though."

"What do you girls get up to at that kind of place, anyway?"

"I've told you before, we go to listen to the music. The bands play there."

"So it's where you hang out. You hang out with all the hookers and drunks down there."

"It's like I said—we don't hang out with those people. We go for the music, that's all."

"What if I don't like you going there all the time? What if I think you could do something more constructive with your time?"

"I go to school full-time. I have a part-time job. What else do you want from me?"

"I want a little respect from you. I want you to get some

normal, decent friends. I want—" She began to cough and couldn't finish what she was saying. Not the first time I'd been grateful for smoker's hack, believe me. I got her a glass of water and left the room, prayed she wouldn't follow me downstairs. She didn't. I got my guitar and called goodbye as I zipped out the back door to go practice at Clare's.

On Monday night I was at work in the downtown Eaton's housewares department. The stores had just started to stay open every night until Xmas and that night it was dead, dead, dead. You could have shot a cannon off and not hit anyone. Got all my homework done, anyway. A night like that on the job just drags. You feel even tireder than if it was busy, I don't know why.

When I finally got home, I went directly into my room. Clare called.

"You've got to turn on the radio right now," she said.

"Why? Is someone we know on CJSW?"

"No. John Lennon's been shot."

"Are you kidding?"

"Would I kid about something like that?"

"I don't know. Who would shoot him?"

I switched on my radio and turned the dial until I found news. The announcer sounded choked up and not very professional.

Entry #28   Wed. 17 Dec. 1980

I can't believe how fucked up I am about John Lennon. I've been so depressed ever since it happened. Nothing seems the same, I've barely even been able to write in here. I guess it sounds weird that the death of someone you never met could affect you like that, but there it is.

Speaking of fucking me up, I saw Niall last night for the first time since The Sisters of Mercy played The Calgarian. This time they played a house party in Lake Bonavista, a birthday bash for some friend of John's. Oh, they were loads of fun and all that, but get this: I could barely make eye contact with him. I felt ashamed somehow, embarrassed, even. Imagine the stupidity. As if I'm the one that has anything to be embarrassed about. Then again, he blushed deeply when we first said hello. Perhaps he does have a conscience, after all.

17

A bunch of us smoked up outside and he came and stood beside me, tried to make small talk. I wanted to ask him, hey, what the hell was that all about last time I saw you, anyway? Of course, I didn't. I was just my usual shy self. A mighty Chinook blew, and sometimes I felt like it might blow me away. It was such a weird feeling. I kept thinking about my own insubstantiality, how I could be blown away and no-one would even notice, least of all him.

Oh, he tried to be nice. But I couldn't bring myself to be friendly back. I guess I was still hurt, still mad. I don't think he realizes at all how bad I've felt. I wondered what good being mad at him would do. But I couldn't help it. Some reptilian part of my brain forced me to give him the cold shoulder. I guess it beat the hell out of screaming at him, which is what I really felt like. He slid his arm around me and even as I felt myself warm to him, I pulled away. One part of me wanted him so badly and the other part wanted to push him away. I felt a new and different kind of empty after I got home, lay in bed and felt all fucked up for hours. Is Ann Landers right, is love just one set of glands calling to another? If so, can I get those glands removed?

On the other hand, I figure this month has just got to start getting better soon. It can't get any worse.

Monday, December 22nd was our last day of school before the holidays. That night we sat at our usual table near the stage in The National and waited for the band to start when a girl ran in through the back door, screaming. We didn't see who it was, we just heard her. Some of her friends took her into the washroom to calm her down, but word spread soon enough: there was a dead body out in the back alley, one of the hookers who'd been out front. Maggie and I looked at each other, said nothing, and both got up to go outside.

A crowd had already gathered around the girl's body when we got there, and we heard the sirens approach. We made our way to the front and people let Maggie by, so I knew before I saw the girl that it was Katya. She looked like she'd just been tossed aside, her white, track-marked arms and fishnet-covered legs sprawled over a pile of snow-covered garbage and broken bottles, on her back with her head hanging down. Her throat had been slashed, and the blood that ran up her neck and out of her mouth into her blond hair looked black in the shadows of the streetlights. I started to cry, felt like I might throw up and put my arm around Maggie. Her shoulders stiffened under my arm, the muscles rippled in her cheek and her nostrils flared as she clenched her jaw. At first I thought maybe she felt sick, too, but she didn't move, didn't say anything.

Three police cruisers pulled over and the cops started to get out. Inside the band had started again, oblivious to what went on outside. The crowd moved aside and the cops approached Katya's body and began to ask us questions. One of them asked if anybody knew this girl.

"I do," said Maggie after a while, in a strange, hoarse voice. "She's my sister."

The police stayed a long time, asked questions, took pictures, put things in plastic bags before they finally took Katya's body away. Maggie went downtown with them. I guess they needed to ask her some more questions, and her parents would probably come down to the police station. I noticed the band had stopped. I don't know if it was because they got closed down, or if their set had just finished. I wondered again where Niall was when he appeared. I hadn't seen him since about 8.30, when he'd disappeared with John. They probably went out to get high or something. Clare said he always fucked off like that because he was a sociopath, had no feelings for anybody else. Just like in that Sex Pistols song, "No Feelings." That must be why his band did it. Anyway, I don't know if he was really a sociopath. Perhaps he was just a jerk.

"What's going on? Are you okay?" he asked.

"Katya. Oh, my God. She's been killed."

"What?"

"Somebody knifed her. A trick, I guess."

"God. That's horrible."

He gave me a ride home. I didn't want to talk much, but Niall started to ask questions. My head pounded, I hardly listened to him anymore. I only wanted to go home and go to bed, and maybe when I woke up, none of this would have happened. Only I didn't think I'd be able to get to sleep, wondered how I could ever sleep again after seeing Katya lying there in the snow.

4. January 1981

We didn't see Maggie over the holidays. I talked to her on the phone a few times and she said her family wanted to have a private funeral for Katya. I would have been happy to be there for Maggie, but that was the way it was. I could understand it. As it turned out, she didn't come back to school until close to the end of January, and then the subject of Katya was closed. Like it had been before only more so. And I just couldn't understand that at all. I wondered why she wasn't madder. If it had been my sister, I would have been outraged. She hardly even seemed bothered by it. How could that be?

Since we couldn't get much out of Maggie, I followed the story in the newspapers. For a couple of weeks after Katya died, they ran stories almost every day. *The Sun* even had pictures of her, wouldn't you know it? Their headline read 'No Clues in Hooker Case'. After a few days the police said they had no leads, and they appealed to the public for information. Before long it was old news, Katya was yesterday's blonde, and you didn't ever hear anymore about it again. After all, the attitude seemed to be, she was just a whore. What does it matter if she gets murdered?

Clare and I went to a New Year's Eve party, but it was pretty sombre. I mean, a lot of people had known Katya. She went to St. Dymphna before she dropped out and now of course, everybody talked about how great she used to be, how nice she used to be, wasn't it awful what had happened to her? What *had* happened to her, I wondered? Not getting killed so much, but everything else. Why did a girl like her, attractive, good student, suddenly drop out of school and start turning tricks out back of The National Hotel? People asked me these things because I was Maggie's friend, because they must have thought I had some special insight into Katya. But I had no clue, nothing. Family was off limits with Maggie, something she talked about as little as possible.

On New Year's Day, Clare and I decided to go to see *Gone With the Wind*, which was playing at The Plaza. I'd seen it once before, when it ran on television for the first time in 1976. I still had vivid memories of the jewel-toned Technicolor and the stunning presence of Vivien Leigh. But when I saw it at age seventeen, it had a whole different impact.

Clare's flame at the time was Andrew, a tall, dark guy who happened to be an usher at The Plaza. He got us in for free on the condition that he could come and join us on his break. We sat in the back as usual and dumped the half-mickey of Southern Comfort Clare liberated from her parents' liquor cabinet into our Cokes.

Right off, I noticed the physical resemblance between Niall and Leslie Howard (though Clare insisted Niall looked more like Danny Kaye). I also saw a parallel between my life and Scarlett's. Obviously, this movie came up at this time in my life for a reason, and Southern Comfort and Coke, which turned out to be not a bad combination, helped me to see that. I barely noticed Andrew when his break rolled around. If I had, I'd have merely found his groping Clare repulsive. "Dirty Yankee," I'd have muttered. As the film unfolded, I identified with Scarlett more and more. Which is exactly why I hated the ending.

"She had Ashley right there in the palm of her hand, just where she wanted him for so many years, and she walked away. I don't understand it," I complained to Clare on the bus on the way home.

"She was in love with Rhett," Clare shrugged. She seemed unaffected by the movie, was no doubt planning her next rendezvous with Andrew.

"But when she finally has the chance to be with Ashley, she realizes she loves Rhett? That makes no sense."

"Okay, Kate, tell you what. Let's have a séance and tell David O. Selznick that Margaret Mitchell got it all wrong. We'll tell him to go back and change the ending because Southern Comfort revealed the truth to us."

"Fuck, Clare, it just didn't seem possible to me."

"Well, I'm not really surprised at that."

Clare quickly figured out my thing for Niall. I denied it at first, but she knew me too well. He didn't impress her much and she wanted to know what I saw in him. What a question. "He's cute," I said. "He's tall, he's funny." I knew I sounded like an idiot but I didn't know what else to say. It was much more than that: he'd touched a nerve, or maybe my spinal cord. After some thought, I added, "He seems necessary to me now. Does that sound ridiculous?" Clare raised her eyebrows. I still didn't know what else to say. Some things can't be explained.

"I don't understand why you don't just tell him how you feel," she said. "If I'm interested in a guy, I let him know right away."

I don't know how she did that. Me, I couldn't, didn't know how or what to say. What if Niall wasn't interested? A lot of times it'd seem like he was, he'd tease me, mess with me. But then he'd go and do stuff like go home with Marianne, or ignore me for weeks at a time. I told myself over and over that I couldn't fall in love with him, that it was stupid, and all the time I knew that it was already too late. I'd decided long ago that marriage wasn't for me, after seeing Carmen and Dad go at it so many times, fighting and screaming and making us all miserable. I didn't want to be stuck in a miserable relationship like my parents. As Catholics, they could never divorce. Perhaps they stayed together for my sake. Gee, thanks.

I couldn't imagine ever bringing a guy home to meet them. Dad on his own was usually okay, but Carmen worried me. Would she be drunk, hungover, asleep at some strange hour? Would she just be sarcastic and hostile? She might even be civil. You never knew what you'd get with her. And until Niall, I'd managed to avoid boys mostly and I hadn't had to worry about these things. But then I had no idea I could ever feel like this about someone. I was losing control, it was out of my hands, it scared the hell out of me.

Once on the packed bus after school, Judith (or Jude, as we started to call her) and I stood and held onto the bar when I spotted Niall and Grace Christie at the back. Grace's boyfriend Tom played bass in Extreme Unction. She wore a nineteen-fifties green wool coat, had her red hair pulled back in a ponytail and her eyeliner done like Elizabeth Taylor's in *Cleopatra*. I shouldn't have felt jealous, I didn't want to. But I did. Clare would scramble over everybody in the bus and plant herself right next to him, up against him maybe. But I just stood still and watched.

"Kate?" asked Jude after a while.

"What?"

"Are you listening?"

"Sorry. I guess my mind was wandering."

Jude turned to the back to see what I'd been focused on.

"Ah," she smiled. "I see. Niall Graham."

I shrugged.

"What is it with you and him, anyway?"

"Good question. It isn't much of anything."

"There are other people around who are a lot more interested in you, you know. People who care about you more than he does."

"Oh, yeah?"

I have to admit I wasn't really listening to her again. Already. The sun was low enough now that it slanted under the chinook arch in the west and lit Niall's green eyes. Grace was five foot nothing and he had to crane his neck down to hear her. What were they saying? After a minute, I realized I was staring and turned away. I searched in my purse for some gum to fight the dryness in my mouth. My eyes turned back to him over and over. Mercifully, my stop came soon.

I said goodbye to Jude, lingered at the bus stop a while, watched the bus pull away. Several times that night, I wondered what Niall and Grace had been talking about. Then as I got into bed, what Jude had said about other people started to register. Other people cared about me? Who? Just then, she called.

"You weren't asleep, were you?" Jude asked.

"No. Funny though, I was thinking about you."

"You were?"

"Yeah. I'm sorry I wasn't listening to you on the bus today."

"That's okay. I could see you were distracted."

"Well, I'm sorry. Anyway, you said something about people who were interested in me. I mean, it didn't really sink in."

"I'm surprised you even absorbed that much of it."

"Aw, give me a break. So are you kidding or what?"

"No."

"Really? Then who do you mean?"

"Me."

"You?" I didn't say anything else for a second. Was Jude kidding?

"Kate?"

"Yeah, I'm still here. Are you serious?"

"Well, yes."

"I don't know what to say."

"You don't have to say anything."

"I guess I'm flattered and everything. But I'm not...you know, I'm not like that."

"It's okay. I just wanted to let you know. Ever since that night I first saw you guys at The National, I've just been thinking about you a lot. I'm very attracted to you."

"That's crazy." After I got off the phone I went to the bathroom, then sat up in bed and smoked for a while. How did all these people tell other people how they felt, just like that? Clare, Jude, probably tons of people did it all the time. How did they do it, and why couldn't I? I mean, if I did that, I'd be on the other end of the phone, cringing. Maybe Jude did cringe. She didn't sound like it, though, she sounded calm. I tried to imagine calling up Niall one night and telling him I found him attractive, and sounding calm and matter of fact while doing it. Nope. Too weird.

And now Jude made me feel even weirder. Jude. I felt confused, flattered, even a bit curious, but it seemed too far out to imagine. I wondered too if I gave off that kind of vibe, sent out some signals without being aware of it. Finally, I laid my head down and turned out the light, although I didn't fall asleep for a while.

Almost as soon as I got out of bed the next day, I wondered again what Niall had been talking to Grace about. It was probably nothing. Something like what some poser had worn to the last show, knowing Grace. I liked her, but she was one of those people who seemed more interested in the fashion part of the scene than anything else. Seemed to me more and more of those types came out to the shows. They got ideas about "punk" music from TV and magazines, and then they'd come to the shows all decked out with spiked hair and safety pins. That was fine, except they also had these ideas about what the music should be like, too. It should be "punk" music, with British accents and swearing and spitting. We didn't all play stuff like that; some bands did, but lots of us played poppier stuff, sixties garage derived stuff. There was even a band or two with keyboards and asymmetrical haircuts who might be described as "New Wave" by those who wanted to compartmentalize. Yet it seemed like more and more of the crowd expected that Sex Pistols/oi kind of thing.

I gulped down my coffee, headed out the door. If I timed it right, I'd catch my bus at the same time Niall transferred onto it from his Mount Royal bus. I scanned the crowd at the stop for him.

What am I doing? I can't let this happen to me.

5. Summer 1979

I first met Niall two summers earlier. The house lights turned down in the standing room only theatre, people talked and jostled in the aisles. A hush fell for a few seconds, then three spots shone on the drum kit and mike stands on stage. Four guys emerged from the blackness, took their places. A driving, repetitive bass line started on its own for a few bars, followed by drums. The tall one with the red guitar and black leather jacket spoke into his mike. "Good afternoon. Welcome to the show. We're XXX."

He stepped back and both guitars started in, loud, ringing, pulsing. Then he stepped back up to the mike and growled, "I got a feeling inside of me, it's kinda strange like a stormy sea...." After they blasted their way through the song I later came to know as The Damned's *New Rose*, the drummer counted off four on his sticks and they started The Ramones'

Blitzkrieg Bop.

I hadn't known what to expect. Clare and Maggie and I had seen the Sex Pistols in the papers and on the TV news. These guys weren't like that. They didn't wear chains or safety pins through their cheeks, they didn't spit or swear. But they weren't like any of the live bands we'd seen before, either. They had no dry-ice machine or synthesizer, none of them had long hair or played Gibson Flying Vs or double-necked guitars. They were clean-cut, wore straight leg jeans and T-shirts, played basic, elemental rock'n'roll. Their energy impressed me: their arms sliced the air around their guitars in frantic Pete Townshend windmills, they jumped all over the stage, they pounded out the songs at a million miles an hour. I'd never seen or heard anything like it. I got caught up in it, had no choice. This music grabbed you by the throat and made you pay attention, whether you liked it or not.

And I liked it a lot. Maggie and Clare bobbed their heads up and down to the music, too. But when the second song ended, it became clear to us why the crowd was so large. We'd been quite impressed before the show as we waited among the throng outside the theatre. These Grade 11 and 12 guys put on the show after school for credit in their music courses, so we didn't think there'd be much of a crowd. St. Dymphna was supposed to be a jock school, and here there were all these people into music. As it turned out, most of the audience came to throw things: garbage and pop cans flew hard and fast at XXX. And strangely, they seemed to enjoy it. They ducked, smiled, thanked the crowd, broke into another number. The crowd broke into a fury and started to storm the stage. Mr. Green, the music instructor, had to pull the band off, and with the help of the vice-principal cleared everyone out of the theatre. We straggled behind, curious to get another look at XXX. But they stayed backstage with Mr. Green and Mr. Behr waved us on.

"Let's go to talk to them," said Clare. That was Clare, all right.

I wasn't so sure about that idea. "Right now?"

"Sure. We can go around to the back. I want to ask the lead guitarist where he got that amp."

Maggie cleaned her glasses like she always did when she was nervous, and gathered up her books. "I've got to go home. See you guys."

Clare was always so much braver than me. She could just walk right up to perfect strangers and talk to them. For me, it was an excruciating experience.

Still, when we got backstage, I was happy I'd come, happy to let her talk. XXX had deeply impressed me, and it wasn't just the music. For one thing, they had a whole new take on unpopularity: they liked it. They'd turned something that had dogged the three of us for ages into a joke. Clare chatted with the red-haired, freckled guitarist, Todd, while I watched the others, drenched with sweat from the stage lights, load up their equipment. I backed against the cinderblock wall, made room for the singer to get by with his guitar case. But he brushed against me anyway. I thought I'd given him lots of room.

"Sorry," he said, and smiled.

"That's okay."

He put his guitar case down. "My name's Niall. Niall Graham."

"I'm Kate Brandt."

I hadn't noticed him around before, probably because he was a year or two ahead of me. Even without the jacket, he couldn't have helped standing out in a crowd with his height. His blond hair was buzzed to within half an inch of his scalp, his eyes were a clear green. He made no attempt to hide his interest as his eyes moved up and down my body.

"Glad you could come to the show today. What did you bring to throw?"

"I didn't know we were supposed to bring anything. But I will next time."

"Check it out, Graham," said Todd. "These girls play guitar."

Niall looked back and forth at Clare and me. "No kidding. So do you have a band or what?"

"Not yet. We're working on it, though," Clare told him. This was news to me. I thought we were just playing guitar.

"That's pretty cool," said Todd.

27

"When do you guys play next?" I asked. I didn't want to get into a discussion of guitar playing, or of the band we were apparently forming. I mean, these guys were in a real band and everything.

"We're trying to get a show together at the Millican-Ogden community hall later in the summer," Niall said. "We'll let you know when we've got it organized. Don't forget to bring something to throw at us."

"What should we bring?" I asked.

"Yourselves."

When we went back to school in September, Todd introduced us to a few other people who listened to punk, maybe eight all together. XXX weren't completely friendless, after all. We thought we might have missed the Millican-Ogden show over the summer, but as it turned out it was planned for the end of September. XXX would open for a band called Extreme Unction.

A few of the people from school were at the hall when Clare, Maggie and I arrived. The place was dark, with long wooden tables lined up around the edges of the room. Most of the other people were older than us. The audience ranged from longhaired freaks and their old ladies to black leather types. Ganja smoke wafted from the back somewhere, and people drank out of wineskins or bottles or Slush cups.

XXX started up and the people from St. Dymphna stood in a knot in front of the stage. They began with *New Rose* and *Blitzkrieg Bop*, like last time. Niall encouraged people to dance, but nobody did. People just stood and watched them, checked them out. Part way through the third song he put down his guitar, jumped off the stage and grabbed my arm. I stood petrified as he pulled at me.

"C'mon. Let's get these people going."

I had to go with him. We started to dance and I wondered if he could see how terrified I was. I'd been nervous enough around all these other, older people and here I was dancing in front of all them. But it worked. After a few seconds, people joined us. When he got back onstage, I was sorry I'd hesitated.

Before long, the shows happened regularly. Clare and I went to all of them. Maggie wasn't allowed out at night as a rule, although sometimes her parents let her, if she got home by 11.30. This meant she never got to see more than the first act. Usually the community hall gigs had two to five bands on the roster, with maybe 150 or so in the audience, the same people all the time. *How many punk rockers does it take to change a lightbulb? A hundred—one to change the lightbulb and ninety-nine on the guest list.*

Funny, but it wasn't much of a stretch for Clare and me to go from listening to sixties bands to listening to these new bands. A lot of the music was poppy and sixties-influenced, or the best of it was, I felt. Bands like The Clash and The Buzzcocks, for instance, had a way with a catchy tune and clever lyrics, didn't just scream obscenities about Nazis and dead babies. Soon we met more people who listened to this stuff, music other than disco and metal. Being part of a community for the first time in our lives was amazing, even if it was a strange little community.

So I guess it was inevitable that we'd go from playing Beatles songs on our steel-string acoustics to saving up and getting electric guitars and amps. Then we started to churn out those power chords, all three of them. I was fine with that. That was enough of a change for me all at once. Clare, though, began to search for a singer, a bass player and a drummer.

I showed up at practice one Sunday afternoon with my hair bleached blond, as light as I could get it in one go. I'd just done it the night before and wasn't used to it yet: every time I saw my reflection, I felt startled. Who was that uncomfortable looking girl? Carmen's reaction had been less than enthusiastic. She'd briefly looked up from her paper and said, "You look like a whore." I bristled about that all the way to Clare's. *Fucking two shades lighter than her, and I'm a whore.*

Practising in the St. Francis' Polynesian-themed basement was always a little surreal, especially in the winter, but after a while, I didn't even see the beach photo mural wallpaper, the grass-mat wall covering, the rattan furniture or the miniature

Tiki gods. Barb, our new bass player, sat in the Papasan chair. She smiled when she saw me. "Whooo-hooo! It's Debbie Harry, everyone."

"Fuck off." I started to wonder how big a mistake I'd made, and whether I should just buzz it all off.

Wendy tried to make me feel better. "Pretty sexy. We could use a blonde out front."

We had a bass player and a drummer. We'd also wanted to find a singer, had one all lined up, but she never did show up at practice, the bitch. So Barb and I decided to handle the vocals ourselves. Now we needed a name. Everybody seemed to have lots of ideas, but we could never all agree on one. I wanted Misscarlett, Clare pulled for Venus in Furs, Barb liked Gun Moll, Wendy liked Stella. We'd each come up with hundreds of names, and none of them stuck. Sometimes it seemed like we spent more time bouncing names around than we did playing music.

Clare took a minute to look at me from all angles.

"Can we cut the shit about my hair and just get busy here?"

"I like it," Clare responded with a grin. "Just wondering why you did it."

I plugged in my guitar, started to tune up. "I don't know. I was bored. Wanted something different, you know." Deep down, I think I hoped that being blond would somehow make me brave, sexy, confident, like the girls on the boxes of haircolour looked. Without question it got you noticed, I was finding that out already. I didn't feel any braver, though.

6. Summer 1980

Clare and Maggie and I were all avid readers. Maggie read Science Fiction/Fantasy stuff. The further away from reality a novel was the better she liked it. She used to rag me about the stuff I read. "What's with you and those *classics*?" she'd ask, like I had a disease or something. I was in the midst of a little

Hemingway phase right then and she couldn't stand him. Maybe there weren't enough alien life forms in *The Sun Also Rises*. Clare was the most voracious of us. She read indiscriminately: Science Fiction, classic novels, raunchy romances, poetry, history, biographies. Cereal boxes when desperate, I'd seen her do it. I wouldn't read a lot of the stuff she did, but she always had some interesting recommendations.

She'd recently turned me on to Anaïs Nin. We both read *Delta of Venus* and *Little Birds*, collections of short pieces of erotica that Nin wrote early in her career, reputedly for a dollar a page for wealthy clients. I found them amazing and started to write some vignettes of my own. Writing was all I seemed to be able to do that was anything like a solution to the problem of my love life, or total absence of one. It wasn't much of a solution, but it was my only way of letting off steam, although sometimes it had the effect of creating more steam than it let off.

Extreme Unction opened for The Subhumans from Vancouver one Friday at Orange Hall and a bunch of us danced to the pre-show tape. During Magazine's *Shot by Both Sides* I noticed a bald, stocky middle-aged man near the back of the room. *"Wormed my way to the heart of the crowd, wormed my way to the heart of the crowd,"* snarled Howard Devoto as the man jostled past dancers. As he got closer I saw that it was Artur Iwaniszyn, Maggie's father. Maggie had said earlier that she wasn't supposed to be there, but she'd snuck out for The Subhumans. He came up behind her and grabbed her by the upper arm, spun her around to face him. She was wide-eyed, pale. She opened her mouth, but before she could speak he slapped her, sent her glasses spinning across the floor into an amplifier stack. Then he turned to leave without a word. She scrambled for her glasses, hastily put them back on and without making eye contact with anyone, followed him out the door.

"What the hell was that? Who was that guy?" Niall asked me.

"That was her father." I didn't know what else to say. Then Extreme Unction started. All hope of further conversation was lost, then. It was too loud.

"Come on outside," Niall said during the set break. "I want to get some fresh air."

For October, the night was warm, warm enough that we didn't need our jackets. We went out the back door and across the parking-lot, over to the bleachers behind the ball diamond, could barely even hear the taped music in the hall. He finished his beer and I had a cigarette while we talked about The Clash show Niall had just seen with some friends in Vancouver. They'd even met the band, got to go backstage with them after the show.

"They were really nice, down-to-earth guys. They had these massive fruit trays all over the dressing-room," Niall said. "And they were drinking Perrier water. Help yourselves, they said."

"They probably wanted to wait until after you guys left to start on the beer. You would have hung around all night if they'd given you beer."

"That could be. But, hey—what's with Maggie's dad?"

"I don't know. He's always been like that, as far as I know. She doesn't talk about her family much. They came here from Poland when Maggie was about ten and I remember she was allowed out after school once a week, to go the library. It's only been in the last couple of years that he's allowed her to go much of anywhere, and I think it's because Maggie's said, well, you kept Katya on a short leash and look what she's doing now. Maybe he's afraid Maggie will end up doing the same thing."

"Jesus, what a psycho. I can just imagine how happy he was about Katya working the National stroll."

"But which came first, you know? If he hadn't been such an asshole, she wouldn't have left home at fifteen and gone out to work the streets in the first place."

"So how does Maggie stand him?"

I looked at him for minute before I answered, tried to think what to say. Niall's dad was a partner in a law firm, his own father's law firm, in fact, Graham Wolff. The Grahams had a big house in Mount Royal. He probably had no idea what it was like to have a parent who was a psycho. Or a drunk.

"Maybe she doesn't have a choice. Maybe she sees Katya and thinks it's better at home. But I don't know. Like I said, she doesn't talk much about it." I knew what that felt like, for sure.

We heard pounding drums and throbbing bass. "Sounds like the band's starting up," I said.

"That's okay. They'll play all night." He slid over next to me and put his arm around me, ran his hand up and down my arm. "Aren't you cold?"

"No. Not right now."

"I like your Elvis Costello button." He must have. He gave it a close inspection.

Suddenly lights flashed and sirens screamed in the parking-lot. "Oh, shit," Niall hissed.

We went back inside the hall. You'd think they were breaking up a major crime ring, not hassling a few punk rockers because of noise complaints. I counted three vans and six cars worth of them, and they played the bad cop act to the hilt. An officer escorted me out the door, my arm bent behind my back, to the parking-lot where another took a statement from Niall, who'd helped to organize the event. Meanwhile other cops who'd confiscated all the booze made a great show of pouring it, bottle by bottle, onto the asphalt. My arm hurt like hell. Niall stepped toward us.

"Excuse me. There's no need for that, is there?"

The cop yanked my arm even harder. "What's that?" he asked. The officer with Niall frowned sharply and I was released. Niall put his arm around me and finished giving his statement. Then he took me aside. "Are you okay?"

"Yeah. Fucking cops. Are they going to charge you with anything?"

"I don't know. I just hope we can pay The Subhumans. This punk rock shit is no fun, eh?"

No, not really, not that part of it. On the other hand, if getting manhandled by cops got Niall to pay attention to me, I had no problem with it.

7. June 1981

On a hot Friday night in June we went to a gig at Millican-Ogden hall. The rest of St. Dymphna's graduating class were at the big celebration up at the Jube, the Jubilee Auditorium, but Jude and I decided to get loaded with our friends instead. Maggie was graduating, too, but it looked like she wouldn't be able to go anywhere for her big night. She'd said she'd try to talk her parents into letting her come with us, but so far there was no sign of her. On the bright side, maybe now that she'd finished school she could find a job and move out. Jude and I sat out on the front steps of the hall to cool off after the first set, drinking Slush with vodka.

"So what are you doing for the summer?" Jude asked.

"I don't know. Probably pretty much what I'm doing now. There's band practice twice a week, more than that when we have a gig on."

"You've had a few lately."

It was true. The Calgary scene was booming, new bands popped up all the time. There were shows every weekend, and Misclairol had opened for a few different headliner acts at The National and The Calgarian and played a handful of hall gigs that spring and summer. We got tighter and more confident, although I still had stage fright something fierce the day of gigs. The weird thing was, I was starting to find that once we got onstage and got going, I enjoyed it more than I ever thought possible. I'd never imagined the adrenalin rush I got from playing, and it was pretty addictive.

"And then I'm working at Eaton's and saving some money for school. Hopefully I'll be accepted in English at U of C for the fall. What about you?" I asked.

"I don't know what I'm doing in the fall yet, but as of Monday I'll be housesitting for the summer. Want to join me?"

"Where are you housesitting?"

"At my cousins' place in Scarboro. They're at school in

34

Switzerland and my aunt and uncle are spending the summer travelling around Europe with them."

"Must be nice. So is this some fancy house or what?"

"It's a nice place. Turn of the century house on Shelbourne Street, all restored. Huge."

"Wow. It sounds cool. I don't know, though. I wasn't thinking of moving out until I have some money saved up."

"Well, it would be free rent. But I know what you're saying. Think about it."

"Yeah. Thanks. I will." It did sound good. Could things get uncomfortable if we lived together, seeing the way she felt and all? Mind you, she hadn't said anything else about that in a long time.

Just as I started to think he wouldn't show, Niall came up the steps.

"Hey, congratulations, grads. Welcome to the big world."

"Thanks. It seems pretty much the same as before," I said.

"Yeah, but now you have a great excuse to get loaded."

"We're already working on that," Jude assured him.

"Mind if I join you?" Join me at the hip, he must have meant, he sat so close. Not that I minded.

"No. So why did you miss the first band?"

"I had advance warning they were shitty. One of these fashion bands. Skinny ties, sunglasses, keyboards, you know."

"Yeah, that sums it up. I wish I got advance warning about these things," I said.

We had a great time that evening. Niall and I hung out together all night, even talked about a film at The Plaza sometime. Nothing had changed between us in the year that had gone by. I still couldn't get my mind off him. He still would flirt and get close up to a certain point and then pull back. Then I wouldn't see him again, for weeks sometimes. It fucked with my mind a great deal. Either there was something wrong with me or he was a dickhead. Clare, Jude and Maggie all voted in favour of the latter. But I wasn't so sure. For one thing, why the hell did I love him so much if he was a dickhead? And if he really was a dickhead, why was he so nice to me most of the time? But then if he was so nice, why did he act like such a dickhead sometimes? It was a conundrum all right, one that I couldn't figure out no matter how much cheap draft I drank. But maybe going to a movie would be the turning point. That was almost like a date, like a commitment.

Eventually someone gave me a late ride home. The next morning—well, closer to the next afternoon, actually—I intended to grab a cup of coffee first thing and head back into my nice, dark, quiet room in the basement to nurse my headache. I'd hoped to avoid my mother, but Carmen waited for me at the kitchen table.

"Why aren't you at work?"

"I traded with Candy for Thursday night, because I knew I'd be out late last night," I said as I scooped coffee into the drip basket.

"And where were you? Do you know you didn't get back here until almost three?"

"I know. I told you, I was at a show at Millican-Ogden hall."

"I suppose Niall was there."

"He was." I was confused. How the fuck did she know anything about Niall? Then she dropped a stack of books onto the kitchen table with a thud. *Delta of Venus, Little Birds.* And, oh Christ, my journal and notebooks. I thought I'd hidden them well enough.

She didn't speak for a while. The look of disgust on her face said it all. She flipped through my notebooks, looked up at me every once in a while, waited for a reaction, perhaps, or an explanation.

"Well?" she asked.

"What do you want me to say?"

"This is pornography. All of it."

"It's not pornography. Those books are erotica. And that other stuff is just my writing. It's—nothing. It's supposed to be private."

"My daughter is writing pornography." I hadn't noticed she was drinking before, but as she slammed my journal down I heard the tinkle of ice in the glass on the table. "Writing pornography and doing God knows what with this Niall.

36

This depraved punk rocker."

"Niall and I are just friends. That's all."

"Oh, right. Don't expect me to believe that. I'm not an idiot."

"Believe what you want. But it's true."

"I won't stand for this. I won't. You write and read this pornographic crap, you carry on with men—"

"I do not carry on with men. It's fiction. It didn't happen, I made it up. And you shouldn't snoop in my stuff."

"I guess I'll damn well snoop where I please in my own house, you lying little bitch. How else would I ever know what you get up to? And now I find this."

My head pounded, I was tired. The coffee finished dripping at last and I poured myself a cup. I couldn't stand seeing her with my notebooks and my journal. I wanted to grab them and run, anywhere. As soon as I finished my coffee.

Carmen continued. "Did you hear what I said? I won't stand for this. I want you out of this house. This is all I'm prepared to put up with from you. Your band, your weird friends, staying out all night, and now you're writing this crap. I've had it."

Oh, right at that moment I would have loved to leave. I'd wanted to leave for years, but I knew going to university meant living at home. There was no way I could afford tuition and rent on my part-time wages at Eaton's, and Carmen and Dad sure couldn't help me. Dad hadn't been able to hold down a job for longer than a few months at a time for years, now. Had Carmen ever worked? I couldn't imagine it.

Jude. Then I remembered—Jude asked me to stay with her for the summer. Oh. Yes.

"Are you listening to me?" she demanded.

I could have said a lot of things to her right then, almost did. Maybe I should have. Maybe I should have said I was sick of the drinking, sick of her putting me down, sick of her not trusting me. Instead I bit my tongue.

"Are you listening?" she asked again.

"I'm listening. And that's fine, I'll start packing now." I gulped down the rest of the coffee in my cup, grabbed my books before she could touch them again and headed down

37

the stairs. There was no point in making her madder. Besides, I'd spent my whole life trying to figure out how not to set her off—I wouldn't do it on purpose now that I was on the verge of escape.

Escape. Just the idea excited me so much I couldn't think about anything else. Well, almost. I spent most of that day and the next getting my stuff organized to move out. Dad tried to talk me out of it, but I had my mind made up. As for Carmen, I think she was surprised into silence. In fact, she didn't even seem to be around most of the time while I packed. She was probably out at the bar. Whatever. I appreciated not having her in my face.

As I packed I came across a black and white snapshot caught in the back of a dresser drawer, probably stuck there since Carmen gave me the dresser when she and Dad got a new one. It was a picture taken on their wedding day, one I hadn't seen in a long time. They stood on a lawn, squinted into the sun, Dad's arm around Carmen's shoulders. Carmen wore a white pillbox hat, a sleeveless white princess cut dress and opaque white hose, Dad wore a dark suit with narrow lapels and a skinny tie. They smiled broadly, looked happier than I'd ever seen them. And it was, what, twenty years earlier? I remembered seeing the picture when I was little and asking Carmen who those people were. She laughed and said, "That's your dad and me. About a million years ago." Whatever happened to that happy, squinting couple? It was like they disappeared and were replaced by my parents. It occurred to me then that they had been young and in love once, too. They must have been. But I could not imagine it.

Jude brought her parents' old Volvo wagon over Monday morning and ferried loads of my stuff over to her cousins' house. I didn't have that much, really. Books and records made up a lot of it, and my guitar, amp, record player and clothes. By noon, we finished. Dad was out at his current job doing the books at a car dealership and we'd said goodbye before he left. Carmen, he warned me, had been out late the night before. She was still in bed and I had no wish to wake her.

I left her a note on the kitchen table, locked the door

behind me and got into Jude's car. I felt incredibly light. And kind of anxious and energized. Maybe even a little scared. But we pulled away from my parents' house, and soon it was just a dot in the rearview mirror.

8. July 1981

The Berg family's house was as amazing as Jude said. It faced west on a quiet, winding street in Scarboro, one of the old money areas of Calgary on the edge of downtown. The upstairs had six bedrooms, and all the rooms had leaded glass windows, high ceilings, elaborate light fixtures, dark wainscoting and hardwood floors. The furniture was all antique and everything was in period colours. At first I was afraid I'd wreck something, but I relaxed after a few days. The bus ride to Eaton's downtown was short and I could play guitar in my bedroom and Jude couldn't even hear me at the other end of the house. The parties we could have had—but we didn't dare. We did have a few people over at a time, though.

We both picked corner bedrooms. Jude got the northwest corner and I got the southwest. Both of them had almost ceiling to floor windows that wrapped around the corners. From my room I had views of Victoria Park and Ramsay, as well as downtown. With a telescope, I might have even been able to see The National.

I didn't need a telescope to see Elveden House, the office building where the Graham Wolff offices were. Niall worked there as a file clerk, had been since he graduated the year before, and was ostensibly saving money to go to school. I always thought he'd go to Alberta College of Art, since he could draw so well. He said he'd thought about that, but hadn't made his mind up yet. Anyway, I could see where a job in your dad's law office wouldn't be too bad. He probably made decent money, didn't have to work too hard, probably didn't have to worry much about missing the odd day or taking a long lunch now and then.

Not long after the move I went to the Eighth Avenue mall at lunchtime, headed west toward Elveden House and sure enough, I ran into Niall. I got a bench and waited for him while he grabbed something to eat.

"So I heard you moved," he said when he came back with some pizza. The sun beat down on us. He must have been hot in his black dress shirt. Even in my sleeveless dress, I felt uncomfortable.

"Yeah, I did. Last week. Jude's housesitting for the summer and I'm staying with her."

"You didn't mention anything about it when I saw you at Millican-Ogden that night. Was it sudden?"

"Kind of. She'd just asked me about it then and I hadn't decided yet."

"So where is this place?"

"It's in Scarboro. Jude's cousins' place. A nice, huge turn-of-the-century house." As soon as I said it, I realized how dumb this must have sounded. What did I think the Grahams' place in Mount Royal was like, a two-bedroom bungalow?

"I'd like to see it sometime."

'Why don't you come over some evening?"

"How's tomorrow?"

"Um, sure. Around 7.30?"

"Great. It sounds really cool."

Holy shit, I thought as I rushed back to Eaton's.

When I got home I went up to my bedroom, put on a record and tried to figure out what I'd wear the next night. Nothing seemed right. It was all either too formal, too casual or fit wrong. I might have to stop in at the Sally Ann on my lunch hour.

Jude knocked on my door. "Are you listening to that fucking Bob Dylan again?" She was mostly razzing me, but I knew Bob drove her nuts. She was just getting heavily into some of the California bands like Black Flag, The Circle Jerks and The Dead Kennedys right then, and I was listening to *Nashville Skyline* almost everyday. I enjoyed the irony of the situation.

"Who would have ever guessed that music would become a sore point between us? Next you'll be banging on the floor of your bedroom when I'm listening to records downstairs. 'Turn that noise down!'"

"Well, if you didn't listen to such *shit*. Bob Dylan!"

"What can I say? Bob just speaks to me." I didn't add that I found bands like Black Flag tiresome and repetitive.

"What are you doing?" she asked, looking at the clothes piled on the bed and the floor behind me. I think I'd tried on almost every piece of clothing I owned.

"I'm trying to figure out what to wear tomorrow night. Niall's coming over."

"No kidding. So what brought this on?"

"I ran into him at lunchtime. God, I have nothing to wear."

"I wouldn't worry about it too much. I'm sure jeans will be fine. Oh, please, can we turn this record off now?"

The song was *Lay, Lady, Lay*. That song got on her nerves, that one and *Just Like a Woman*.

"I'll turn it down a bit, but I happen to like this song. Sorry."

"Eww. I mean, what is with his voice in this song? What is that?"

"That's his *Nashville Skyline* voice. C'mon, sing along...*and you're the best thing that he's ever seen.*"

"Yeah, exactly. You *are* the best thing he's ever seen. So don't freak yourself out over what to wear."

"Shit, I am not freaking out. I just don't have anything to wear."

"Whatever you say. I'm going downstairs to find something to eat."

"Okay. I'll be down in a minute."

Our friend Mike Watson, a tall, thin, dark-haired guy, came by to pick up Jude shortly after six the next night. They were going to *Monty Python and the Holy Grail* at The Plaza.

"Hey, Kate. How are you?"

"Oh, I'm good," I lied. I was nervous, thought about catching a bus somewhere and letting this night not happen.

41

Or letting it happen without me, anyway.

"Where did you take off to last week when we were at The Calgarian?"

"I had a headache. I went home early."

Jude came down the stairs just then. "I thought you left because you thought Niall wouldn't show," she said.

"Yeah?" asked Mike. "He came later. He was looking for you."

"Really? Huh." *He was looking for me?*

"We'd better go, Mike," said Jude. "But you two have fun tonight. And don't worry, I won't be back until late."

"Yeah. Well, you have fun, too."

As I watched them walk out the front gate I wondered again about Jude. She hadn't mentioned anything about her feelings for me again since that night we talked about it on the phone. And now the last little while she and Mike seemed inseparable. I felt a little bad for wondering whether there would be trouble between us. Obviously, she'd forgotten about it.

I wasn't watching for Niall out the front window. Really, I was watching the weather. The sky was almost black to the west and there'd been a few rumbles of thunder in the distance. I'd only been ready since 6.30, finally deciding on jeans, a black belt and a form-fitting black shirt with a deep v-neck. Since then I'd moved around the house, straightened things out. Things near windows, mostly. When the doorbell rang I wished Jude was there to answer it, so I could maybe hide or run out the back door. Why did I feel like I had stage fright? Well, it wasn't that bad. I didn't feel like I might throw up, much. My hand was on the doorknob when I suddenly wondered if I had too much perfume on, but it was too late. I opened the door.

Niall wore jeans, too, and a black T-shirt. He smiled at me. "Hi."

"Hi, Niall. Come in. Is it raining?"

"Yeah, a little. I brought this," he said, and handed me a bottle. "I don't know if you like red wine."

"Red wine is fine. Thank you."

"You look great."

"Thank you. So do you." And he did. His hair was still a little damp from the shower, and he'd just shaved. I wanted to run my fingers along his jaw, but took a deep breath instead. Was it my imagination, or was he a little flushed?

"Thanks. So, how about a tour?"

"Sure."

It was weird living in a place big enough to give our guests a tour. At my parents' place in Spruce Cliff, the tour would have been given by standing in the kitchen and pointing— there's the living-room, there's the bathroom, there's my parents' room and my room's in the basement. But this house had a parlour (we spent a lot of time there, since that's where the stereo was), a den, a full bathroom, a kitchen, a dining-room, and a walk-in pantry on the main floor. Upstairs had a sitting-room and another bathroom as well as the bedrooms.

"Is this your bedroom?" he asked as we stood in the doorway.

"Yeah." I was embarrassed all of a sudden, glad he could have no idea what I'd been thinking night after night, lying in that big, beautiful bed. Or did he? He smiled at me, watched for a reaction, maybe? I had to look away. "Nice view, eh?"

"No kidding. It's a great room."

"Yeah, I've been enjoying it. So, uh, that's it. That's the whole house."

"Well, that was exhausting. I think I need some of that wine."

"Me, too."

I found some glasses and a corkscrew in the kitchen while he flipped through the records in the parlour. He put on The Byrds, another band Jude hated. I guess they're pretty Dylanesque, come to think of it. He sat close to me on the green brocade couch and we touched glasses.

"Cheers," I said.

"Cheers. So what's new?"

"Besides moving out? Not much. I'm working. We prac-tise a lot. We're supposed to play with Dog-Faced Boy and

43

some other band in a few weeks. What about you guys? I haven't seen The Sisters around much lately."

"Yeah, I don't know. We have fun together but I think we've started to diverge. John is really into the hardcore stuff and I've lost interest in it. And Hammerhead's just Hammerhead, you know?"

"Sure. That hardcore stuff gets old fast, doesn't it?"

"It does. And it seems like that's all the newer bands are about."

"Well, there's a demand for it."

"There is. But where does that leave us?"

"Out in the cold, again. It's not a surprise when you think about it. It was only a matter of time before popular demand took over. I mean, look at the way people vote here—we've had the Conservatives in power for ten years, for Christ's sake. It's the group mentality thing. This is good wine, by the way."

"It's from my dad's wine cellar. So I guess before, the group wasn't big enough to have a group mentality."

"Maybe before it was so small it had to tolerate diversity. But now there's a lot of these skinheads and skaters around."

"Kind of depressing, isn't it?" he asked.

The wine went down easily at this point. Before long he refilled our glasses. This time he came up with a toast, a little more thoughtful than mine had been. "To old friends."

I had a sip of wine. "I guess we are old friends. We've known each other, what, a couple of years? Three years?" I tried to sound like I had no idea how long I'd known him. I knew practically down to the second.

"A couple of years, anyway. And I understand you've been interested in me for quite a bit of that time."

I felt my face go hot. "You knew?"

"I've had some ideas. And certain people have told me the last little while."

Who, I wanted to know? But it didn't matter, really. It could have been any number of people. I swallowed. "It's true." He moved closer, eyes scanned my face, lingered on my eyes. I stared at his long eyelashes and moved closer to him. He slid his hand over mine.

44

"Your hands are so cold."

"I'm really nervous."

"You don't have to be nervous. Have a sip of your wine."

I did. It didn't help.

"Just relax," he said.

The silence was so deep I wasn't even sure, just then, if either of us were breathing. I took a deep breath and leaned toward him. He leaned in closer and tilted his head a little and kissed me, gently at first. I tasted smoke and red wine and National Hotel draft on his lips. After a little while I felt the tension melt out of my body, felt myself able to breathe deeply. I began to relax and let him pull me closer. I caressed his shoulders, his back, his chest and he lowered me onto my back. I peeled his shirt off and he peeled mine off. As he admired my black satin bra, the needle started to pop in the groove at the end of the record. I couldn't stand that, and got up to fix it.

"Everything okay?" he asked.

I put the tone arm in its holder, turned the stereo off, and slid back beside him on the couch. "Everything's fine. Great."

With the music gone, I noticed the rain drum on the roof. Then a flash of lightning lit the room for a second, followed almost immediately by a low, rumbling crash.

"That was close," I whispered, and dug my fingers into him.

"Are you afraid of lightning?"

"A little."

"Don't worry. I won't let anything happen to you."

I wasn't actually worried about anything happening to me. On the contrary, I hoped it would, and it seemed more and more urgent as we explored each other that it should. I had been so afraid that when this really happened, when we finally touched, kissed, explored each other, that it couldn't possibly be as amazing as I imagined. So far so good, though. I started to open the button on his jeans and he obviously felt the same way. Then he pulled back a little, breathed out slowly.

"We should stop," he sighed. "I don't want to. But I think we should. Stop, I mean." He didn't sound quite convinced, his hands still moved slowly over my thighs. I was a little con-

45

fused at first, but then the light went on. First date. Good girl.

Right. Now why didn't I think of that?

"I guess you're right," I said. Wasn't there some kind of special dispensation for people who'd already known each other a long time? People who were old friends? I got up and found my bra and shirt and started to put them back on.

He came up behind me and put his arms around me. "Listen," he said, "Don't take it the wrong way. I want to finish this with you, soon."

I kissed him. "It's okay. I understand."

I understood in a way. We had to play by the rules, I guess. I hadn't seen this side of Niall before, hadn't known it existed. The things you learn about people when you make out with them.

The wait seemed like forever, but it was actually the next weekend that I met Niall to check out bands at The National. It was all I could do the whole time to keep my hands off him. He seemed equally impatient. After the first band finished (whoever they may have been; I paid no attention) he suggested we leave.

We got into his old blue Volkswagen, his dad's cast-off. At the house we sat out on the swing on the back verandah with the lights turned off and smoked a joint. He slid over close to me.

"Where's Jude at tonight?" He ran his fingers along my neck and collarbone and shoulders. I wore a strapless green brocade sheath and I think he found it intriguing.

"She went to a movie with Mike."

"Will she be out late?"

"I don't know. Maybe."

"Maybe we'd better go right upstairs."

Although I couldn't wait to be alone with him, I was also nervous as hell. We climbed the stairs and went into my room. I closed the door and took a deep breath. He pulled me up against him and I stood on tiptoes to reach his mouth. We stood like that for a long time, bodies pressed up hard against each other, mouths hungry, almost forgetting to breathe.

"Christ, that was a long week. Wasn't it?" he asked as he led me to a chaise longue near the window.

"It was fucking hell."

I'd managed to dig up some black silk stockings for the occasion and his hands ran appreciatively up and down the smoothness of my legs as I leaned back. Then they moved up to my back. He unzipped my dress and slid his hand slowly inside. After a while I stood and he slipped the dress off. He inhaled audibly as it fell to the floor. "Oh, Jesus," he whispered, stroked my breasts gently, kissed them. I slipped off his shirt and covered his chest with hot, slow kisses. His fingers slid under the black garters, pressed into my thighs, china white against the burgundy upholstery. He eased me onto my back and I ran my fingers through his thick waves of blond hair, caressed the back of his neck as he nibbled my belly.

"I thought about you a lot. I thought about doing this a lot. Are you ready?"

"Ready? Am I ready?" I laughed. "What do you think?" He stood and I unzipped his jeans. They dropped onto the Persian rug under our feet. Finally we stood naked in the dim glow from the streetlights.

"I think you may be ready," he said. "I'm ready."

"I can see that."

"Jesus," he gasped as I pulled him onto the bed.

Whatever reservations or hesitation he'd had the week before were a dim memory. We spent the night making love until we dozed off, then we'd wake and start over again, maybe have a glass of wine. Then the room started to get light. I had my ear against his chest, listened to the pounding, unable to move.

"I could keep at this all night, you know," he said, and twirled a finger in my hair.

"I'm getting that idea. I mean, it's not night anymore."

"That's true. Where does the time go? So, how do you feel?"

"I'm fine. Except I'm tired. And tomorrow I'll probably be stiff in a few places."

"Today, you mean."

47

"I don't know what I mean. Whatever. I have to go to sleep now."

"Me, too. Goodnight."

9. August 1981

Those days at the Bergs' house were some of the happiest days of my life. For a while. July was a fantastic month. Niall and I were together as often as we could manage it, up in my room much of the time. I'm sure I drove people nuts, humming tuneless little tunes, smiling for no reason and spending hours on the phone with him. It annoyed the hell out of Jude. "Maybe I might get a call once in a while if the line wasn't always busy," she said. "And what do you two find to talk about all that time anyway?"

But things seemed to go bad in a hurry. First, I realized I couldn't afford to go to university in the fall. If I really cut corners, I might be able to start in January, but more likely I'd start in the fall of '82. I was disappointed at first, but realized after a while that it was probably better to work for a year or so anyway. And then suddenly Niall wasn't home when I called. I left messages with his mom a couple of times, but he didn't call back. When I called again there was no answer at all. I didn't see him at The Calgarian or The National. I didn't see him for three weeks. I was almost out of my mind. Had he found someone else? Was he mad at me? I couldn't imagine what had happened. I spent a lot of time up in my room, supposedly reading *For Whom the Bell Tolls* and talking to Maggie on the phone. Then one Sunday night he showed up at our door.

"Where have you been?" I asked.

"Toronto, the last two weeks. Remember?"

"You didn't tell me."

"Didn't I? My parents and I were out there visiting my uncle."

48

"I've been trying to call you, and I had no idea where you were or anything."

"I'm sorry. I thought I told you."

What about the week before that, I thought. *Why didn't you return my calls?* But I didn't want our relationship to become possessive, where we both had to know what the other did all the time. I'd seen and heard enough disputes between my parents about that kind of shit. I had no wish to live my life like that. Still, something else made me want to know where he was and what he did. And yet I didn't want that to matter to me. What the fuck was that all about?

"Can I come in for a while?" he asked. "I missed you."

"I missed you, too."

It felt so good to have my arms around him again, I almost didn't care about being mad at him. What did it matter, after all? He was here, now. The rest, I could forget.

At the end of August we did have one small party, a moving-out party, and invited just a select few friends who could be trusted not to trash anything or vomit on the upholstery: Mike, Clare, Barb, Wendy, Maggie, Niall, Dave and a couple of others. Around midnight I noticed Maggie was still around, and she was usually long gone by about eleven or so. Kind of weird, I thought, but maybe now that she was done school her parents were easing up on her a bit.

"Hey, Maggie, if you want to crash here tonight, there's lots of room," I told her.

"Yeah, I might do that. Could I talk to you alone for a while?"

"Sure."

I refilled our glasses of Asti Spumante and we headed up to my room. Something big must have been up, I knew, and it felt a little funny. She hardly ever seemed to want or need to talk about things. She'd listen to me go on about Niall for hours on the phone at night. She'd usually tell me he really did love me, he was just an immature asshole. But she'd hardly ever talk about her troubles.

We sat down on the bed and Maggie looked around. "This is a beautiful room. I bet you'll miss it," she said.

49

"Yeah, I will. I'll probably never have a room like this again. But at least I had it for a while."

"You're lucky. And that's kind of what I wanted to talk about. I need to move out, and I wondered if I could stay with you guys for a while."

"I'll have to talk to Jude, but I don't see why not. The new place we've got in Vic Park is big. I think that would work fine."

"Thanks, Kate. But you're not moving until next weekend. Do you think it would be okay if I stayed with you here until then? Like, starting now?"

"Well, sure. I'm sure Jude won't mind. Is something wrong?"

She hung her head, wouldn't look at me. "You know my parents," she started.

"They're really strict. And your dad can be unreasonable."

She flashed a look at me. "That's one way of putting it. I mean, you know all the stuff about no boys, no makeup."

"I always think it's pretty good how you manage to put your makeup on riding the bus. That takes a steady hand."

"Yeah, well, all that stuff. No staying out late, no going out on Sundays. I hated it, but I could stand it as long as Katya was around. Then when she left, my dad started...."

She trailed off and I wasn't about to try to finish that sentence. The longer the silence grew, the more I didn't want to find out the rest of it. Her father had given me the creeps ever since he came up their back stairs behind us once and made a remark about Clare's tight jeans. I put my hand on Maggie's tense shoulders and she started to quake gently. I realized that in all the time I'd known her, I'd never seen her cry before. I wanted to cry myself.

"You can tell me, Maggie. You need to tell someone."

She held onto me then and wailed for a good long time, and I wished I could think of something good to say. But I couldn't. I just held on too, and told her to go ahead and cry. Then I felt ashamed that I'd spent so much of Maggie's time with my petty problems when she had this in her life. Why didn't I have some idea? But she'd never said a word about it before.

50

After a while she calmed down enough so that she could speak again. She had a fair swig of wine and took a deep breath. "You know," she said. "I called Katya one night right after she moved out because I didn't know why she'd left. I was mad at her. I was mad at her for leaving me alone. And then she told me why she left. She said I'd better leave soon, too, before he started with me. And you know how stupid I am? I didn't believe her. I thought she was crazy, maybe she was making it all up. And then, not even a month after she moved out, he started to come to my room in the middle of the night. And after she died…I thought he might leave me alone, even for a while. But it was almost worse after that."

"Oh, Maggie. I'm so sorry."

"And that isn't even the worst part of it. I mean, I'm tough. I am. I thought if Katya could handle it, I could, at least until I finished school. And then I could get a job and move out. But now that school's done he won't let me get a job. He doesn't want me to leave."

"You have to."

"I know. I am. My cousin works in a bank, and she thinks she can help me get a job. I go in on Monday to see them."

"That's good. See? You'll have a job next week, and we'll be in the new house next weekend. Things will get better. You don't deserve to take that kind of shit."

She looked me straight in the eye. "You don't deserve to take shit either, you know."

"Don't worry about me. I'm fine," I told her, ashamed that she'd even think of me at such a time.

We stayed in my room and talked a little while longer. Maggie fixed her makeup and hugged me once more and we came back downstairs, where people drank and listened to music as if nothing had happened.

The next morning Maggie called home to let them know she was okay and all, and I guess they were just freaking. Kind of funny how I got kicked out of home and she ran away. Neither of us could just amicably move out of our parents' homes by mutual agreement at some convenient time. I wasn't there when she went back to pick up her things, coward that I am.

10. September 1981

Our 1912 two-storey wood frame house sat on 12th Avenue, Victoria Park's main drag. Built in the height of Calgary's first boom, it must have been a fine-looking home in its day. But Vic Park had been the wrong side of the tracks since at least World War II and was being converted, house by house, block by block, into more parking for the Stampede. Never mind that the house's 30-year-old paint job was bleached pale yellow and pink, never mind that we had to watch for syringes in the yard. For Maggie, Jude and me, it was perfect. Nowhere else could we have found an entire 1200 square foot house for only $125 each per month. And on the corner of a busy street, with a corner store behind, an empty lot on one side and an alley on the other, we could practice day and night and no-one cared, no-one bitched, no-one called the cops with noise complaints. We loved it.

We set up our equipment in the basement, concrete studded with smooth river rocks, punctuated by three tiny windows. The main floor had the kitchen and a huge sitting-room with a tall bay window and sliding doors off the dining-room, lavishly appointed with cast off rec-room furniture donated by the Morrisons, in an attractive lime green and orange motif. The upper floor had a long hall with a bathroom at one end, three bedrooms and a linen closet along the sides, and my room at the other end.

My room wasn't really a bedroom, but one of those second-storey sunrooms often seen on homes of that vintage.

The moment I saw it, I said, "I want that room."

"Go ahead," Maggie said. "It's going to be cold."

"I know."

"It doesn't even have a closet," said Jude.

"I know. I don't care. I love it anyway." This gave me pause to reflect on the pattern that seemed to be arising in my life: I seemed to have a weakness for things nobody else wanted.

I loved practising in the basement. On hot days it was cool

and a little damp. I thought about how those round river rocks started out somewhere in the Rockies, made their way down the Bow River, thought about smelling 70 years worth of dust. We spent a lot of time down there, and I spent even more time down there by myself, writing lyrics. I'd never been a great guitarist, but I could write lyrics. So Clare came up with the tunes and I took care of the words, generally. We got a lot of gigs in this period, too. We didn't make much money but we played a whole lot, improved a whole lot. Writing and performing our own songs helped me to transform anger and frustration into passion. I'd discovered a way to throw myself into my feelings and make something with them.

One Sunday night as we wrapped up a practice, Niall showed up. I was changing a broken string and didn't notice him descending the stairs. More and more he was just showing up, not calling first. It made me uneasy. I never knew when or if he'd be around, didn't seem to have any say in it.

"Hey, good-looking," Wendy breathed into her mike. I looked up, expecting to see her boyfriend. Instead I saw Niall and my face burned as if I stood there naked. Funny, I often felt like that when he looked at me. "Don't let me bother you. Nobody came to the door when I rang, so I let myself in."

"We've got a couple more songs to run through," I explained. "But I'm glad you came." I always felt like my eyes could have turned into little cartoon hearts when I saw him. Maybe they did, come to think of it. I never looked. When it came to him, it didn't matter how I tried to be logical, practical, reasonable. Often I wished I could have a lobotomy, excise the evidently quite large Niall region of my brain. Life would have been so much easier, so much more enjoyable.

"We're *all* glad you came, Niall. We're tired of practicing, anyway," Wendy added.

I turned to her. "We've got a couple more songs to run through, and then we'll be done."

He sprawled on the old brown couch at the bottom of the stairs. "Sure. Take your time. Just pretend I'm not here."

Just pretend you're not here. Right. "How about if I just pretend Wendy isn't here?"

53

Practice was effectively over then, for me at least, since I couldn't keep my mind on music. He seemed to think he could barge in on whatever I was doing, anytime. Why did I let him? Why didn't I just tell him to go away, I was busy?

Maggie just seemed to bloom once she got away from her parents house. In short order she had a real transformation, a physical one. She went from skinny girl with braids to total knockout. She started to wear makeup all the time, not just when we went to the bar, and got a chance to perfect her technique with it. In preparation for an upcoming night at The Calgarian she did her hair a couple of shades darker, a glossy, deep chestnut. It looked great. I only hoped she felt as good as she looked. Derek, Niall's old buddy from XXX, was bound to sit up and take notice of her now.

Derek Symons was the cute one in XXX, the drummer, the one everybody wanted (everybody except me, of course). He had orange gold hair, green eyes framed with long gold lashes. Great cheekbones, like David Bowie. Tall, wiry, usually wore a leather jacket and jeans. Maggie had it for him bad, but could never work up the courage to even say hello. That night, the story was entirely different. The Calgarian that night was like Maggie's debut. I was a Calgarian Debutante. There was a song there somewhere, I was sure.

She borrowed one of my favourite dresses, a fitted sage green velvet fifties number with three-quarter length sleeves, a square neckline and a row of tiny covered buttons down the front. Annoyingly, it fit her better than it did me (I hadn't worn it in a while because it was a wee bit tight). She looked sensational in it, and her new look gave her a confidence I'd never seen in her before. Derek noticed her. Many men noticed her that night, including Niall, I noted bitterly. Maybe it was the dress. He always did like that dress. Fortunately, Maggie only had eyes for Derek and they took a long, romantic stroll down the Seventh Avenue strip outside The Calgarian, past the hookers and the drunks. It must have been an hour or more later when they came back and they were inseparable for the rest of the night.

Actually, they were inseparable for a long time after that, too. A few months later, Maggie moved in with Derek, and

Wendy moved into her old room. He argued that there was no sense in her paying rent when she could live with him rent-free. He made good money as a welder's apprentice, they'd be fine, he insisted. And Maggie's cousin had found her a part-time bank-teller position and Derek's apartment was not far from her branch. But mainly, they couldn't stand to be apart.

"Oh, thank God," Jude said when I told her Maggie was moving out. "Her room has looked like a landfill since she moved in here. It drives me nuts." If the mess had stayed in her room it wouldn't have been so bad, but she seemed to leave a trail of half-eaten food, clothing and cosmetics (her new obsession) everywhere she went. Jude, on the other hand, was always orderly, neat.

"I didn't really realize how little you two had in common until she moved in. I also didn't realize how messy she is." I said. "I try to ignore it as much as possible. I guess she can't help being a shade eccentric what with her home life."

"I know she's got problems. I still say it's no excuse for being a slob."

Maggie and Derek were never far from each other, no matter where they were. They constantly gazed at each other, touched each other, limbs intertwined, in their own little universe, oblivious. I always thought of Donne: *Nothing else is.* Sometimes I wondered what it would be like to be in a John and Yoko kind of relationship like that. Despite being madly in love with Niall, I wasn't so sure I'd want to be draped around him at all times, and was certain he'd never dream of it. "Someone get a hose," Jude would say. "They're like a couple of dogs!" Lucky for her, they soon didn't get out much anymore and became a couple of homebodies, tied down by work and sheer lust. I was happy for Maggie, though. Let her hang all over him, I thought. She deserved to be happy for a change.

11. August 1982

Maggie dropped by Eaton's as I got off work one evening.

"Hey, guess what? I've been accepted in Accounting at SAIT this fall," she said.

"Cool, Maggie. You're going to be pretty busy, though."

"Yeah, between that and my hours at the bank I'll be busy for a couple of years. But I'm really excited about it. You want to walk over to Chinatown for a bite to celebrate?"

I have to admit I was a little jealous that she'd be studying at the Southern Alberta Institute of Technology in the fall, and I'd still be working at Eaton's. I hadn't saved up much money yet, in spite of our cheap rent. The money I made at Eaton's just wasn't enough that I could think about going back to school, and with the recession on I couldn't get any more hours with them, never mind find another job. If only I could have used the beer Misclairol often got paid in to pay my tuition.

"How's everything?" I asked as we waited for our noodles to arrive. "I mean, how do you feel?" Maggie seemed so different since she moved in with Derek. Good different, mostly. She seemed solidly grounded in life, purposeful, happy. No longer was she the eccentric pariah, awash in her dreams, that she used to be. Yet, for all that, I sensed that something was lost. Though that wasn't necessarily a bad thing. Maybe it was just the weirdness missing. I couldn't be objective, I'd known her for too long.

"Fine. What do you mean?"

"I don't know. It just seems like you've been so busy you probably don't even have time to think about how you feel. You know, about your parents and stuff."

"It's okay. I get angry sometimes. But you're right, maybe I do keep it out of my mind on purpose. Maybe I do stay busy so I don't have to think about it."

"Do you ever think about counselling?"

"Yeah. It might be a good idea. I should look into it sometime."

After dinner, she offered to drive me home in Derek's orange Pinto sedan. Almost as soon as she left her parents' house, he taught her to drive. She'd had her licence since January, so I took her up on her offer. She didn't drink and drive, had nothing to drink at dinner. Neither did I. We were both sober as judges. But maybe I should have had a drink, I thought, as we careened down Twelfth Avenue, perhaps a double or two. Maggie went through orange lights, cut people off, took insane chances. In a Pinto, yet—was she trying to get us blown up or something? We managed to make it back to my place in one piece, though, and she came in for a while.

"I'm happy for you, Mag, for the way things are turning out for you. But you know, before this last year or so, I never would have pegged you as the accounting type. I could never even have imagined you working in a bank. You just seemed too flighty," I confided.

She smiled. "I know. I've changed a lot in the last little while. It's Derek, you know. He's so serious and hard working, it just kind of rubs off on you."

"Maybe I ought to move in with him for a while."

"I'll never give you the chance. Here's the guy you should move in with," she nodded at the front window. Niall came up the front walk.

"We were just talking about you," she told him.

"Were you? About how wonderful I am?"

I coughed. "Something like that."

He turned to me. "Kate. I'm disappointed to find you've been keeping things from me."

"What's that?"

"I heard you guys are opening for DOA in a couple of weeks."

"Don't remind me. I haven't said anything because I think I'm still in denial." My hands felt cold just thinking about it.

Misclairol and DOA. A marvel of misbooking, as far as I could see, almost as bad a matchup as the rockabilly band Clare and I saw open for Black Sabbath. I felt a little sick as we watched the trio die out there. Those headbangers weren't there to hear *Twenty Flight Rock.* The poor bass player tried to clean the garbage splattered all over his vintage stand-up bass, then they were mercifully taken off after three songs. I found the whole thing chilling. Clare didn't seem to think there'd be any problem with us opening for DOA, though, and neither did Barb. Wendy had never even heard of DOA. I don't know, maybe I was just paranoid.

DOA came from Vancouver, and were probably the best-known Canadian punk band, one of the first I heard referred to as "hardcore." Jude loved that stuff: DOA, Black Flag, The Circle Jerks. Sure, I liked DOA, too. It just wasn't the stuff that moved me. Our set had changed since our first gig at Oddfellows Hall. We had more originals, up to ten now, that Clare and I wrote. We covered Dylan's *Positively 4th Street,* The Buzzcocks' *Autonomy,* The Electric Prunes' *I Had Too Much to Dream Last Night.* I imagined the hardcore crowd's reaction to Misclairol's chiming wimp-rock tunes.

"You and your stage fright, Kate," Barb scoffed. "Get over it already."

And things actually weren't too bad when we first arrived at The Calgarian that Friday night. DOA seemed like a bunch of nice enough guys, contrary to the image they projected. Our sound check went well, which made me feel better. Then the crowd started to arrive.

The night was cool and rainy, and before long the place began to smell of wet leather, an improvement on the usual smell. DOA was a big draw, people wanted to get there early to get a good seat. Opening acts didn't usually pack them in, but this time it looked like we'd play to a full house. Many faces were unfamiliar, and I realized as I looked around at the spiked hair, the chains and the dog collars that Calgary's scene had definitely diverged. And I couldn't help but think we were on the wrong side of the fence, the much smaller side. In fact, it amazed me how quickly the anti had become the establishment. The scene reminded me of Alberta politics: everybody went for the same thing all the time. People seemed to have an idea that punk rock was all about fuck off and throwing up on old ladies and that whole shtick. The broader sense of 'punk' meaning stuff like The Troggs and

Iggy Pop and The Modern Lovers seemed to have no validity anymore. Fortunately, the usual big group of tables sat pushed together up front, crowded with our friends, Niall nowhere among them. I guessed he was probably with Jason Ryan again up at CJSW, the campus radio station.

Jason was an old friend of Niall's, a sociology major who seemed to be taking a long time to finish his undergraduate degree. He was a tall, lanky guy, olive skinned, with deep-set black eyes and dark brown hair that had already started to recede. On his weekly CJSW show, he would remind his dozens of listeners that he'd been into bands like The Heartbreakers and The New York Dolls since 1976. I didn't have much use for him, although many of the gals were taken with him, uninterested as he seemed in them. I held out little hope that Niall would show up at all, even though he said he wanted to come. What did that mean, I wondered? If he wanted to come, wouldn't he just come?

Before we knew it, we were up. I downed a quick drink before we got on stage. The Calgarian's tiny stage seemed different, even tinier, I don't know why. Maybe the huge throng that had turned out for DOA, with many faces I'd never seen before, made things feel crowded. Even so I felt good, pretty relaxed during the first song, *Autonomy*. Our friends cheered, the others were polite. The next song was an original and while we still got applause from our friends the rest of the room ignored us. I didn't mind being ignored, but after we played *Positively 4th Street*, things started to get ugly. What else could we do, though, but continue? If we let them see we were scared, they'd destroy us. They're like dogs, I thought— they can smell fear.

During *I Had Too Much to Dream Last Night*, a half-empty beer can hit Barb's mike stand and rolled harmlessly away. Now terror stiffened my body. I looked over at Clare, who was a ghostlier shade of white than usual, frozen to the spot. Then another can hit the stage, and another. No-one got hit, though I got splattered with beer. We finished the song, and the two sound guys came up to talk to us. Joe, our big friend who drummed for Long Gone Daddy, sought out the can throwers. Meanwhile, the yelling and the catcalls got louder.

This was bad. Weren't we all supposed to be on the same side, once? The order was rapidly fading.

"How many songs left?" asked one of the sound guys.

"Six," I answered, as I tried to cower behind them. "Do you think we should play them?"

"Sure. No problem. Play them all. I bet you'll get an encore."

I thought he was being funny. But when he stepped away I saw a gigantic, bearded man, long hair pulled back in a pony-tail, who stood silently in front of Barb's mike. His beefy arms were folded in front of him, and he waited for the audience to quiet. Then I noticed the back of his leather vest: *Hell's Angels*, it said. From the back of the barroom, through the doors that led up to the hotel rooms, came seven more Angels. They stood side by side in front of the stage, silent, arms folded, and stared straight ahead.

Clare came over to whisper in my ear. "Hey, cool. This is just like The Stones at Altamont."

"I hope that doesn't mean they'll kill someone."

"I don't know. I can think of a few likely candidates."

The biker on the stage took Barb's mike, miniature in his massive hand. "You stupid fucks wanna see DOA?" he bel-lowed. The crowd quieted instantly.

"All right, then. Misclairol here is going to finish their set, first. Any objections?"

No-one made a sound. The Angel nodded to us and joined his companions in front of the stage. We started our next song. Afterward, the Angels applauded and the audience fol-lowed.

"This is great," Barb said. "We need these guys around all the time."

The rest of the set went off without a hitch, and we did get an encore, thanks to DOA's security team. Finally, we left the stage and made our way over to our friends. In all the excite-ment, I didn't notice Niall among them. He stood up and put his arms around me.

"I didn't see you come in," I told him.

"I got here right about the time the beer cans started flying. Are you okay?"

"Oh, yeah. Just a little wet. Too bad it wasn't a wet T-shirt contest. I guess it was kind of fun. Well, maybe not fun. Exhilarating? I never would have thought, before now, that I'd be glad to see a biker in here."

DOA put on a fast and furious show after the break, played all their big hits at maximum volume: *Royal Police, Disco Sucks, Woke Up Screaming*. The crowd loved them and got into some serious slam dancing before long. I got out of the way when that started; I'd known too many people who'd got cracked ribs and black eyes slam dancing. After DOA finished for the night they invited Misclairol and a few others to party with them in their deluxe room upstairs. Wendy, as usual, had taken off right after our set but the rest of us went with DOA. I'd never been in any of The Calgarian's rooms before. An incoherent man in an undershirt and boxer shorts staggered down the hallway where bare lightbulbs dangled from the ceiling and the reddish-orange shag carpet smelled of urine and vomit. DOA's dingy, sour-smelling room seemed quite pleasant in comparison, at first.

"Nice window," Niall said, and pushed a jagged shard out of a pane.

"That's nothing," said Mike, one of the Angels. "Wanna see something really gross? Check out this bed."

He peeled back the covers and lifted a corner of the thin blue and white striped mattress. The box spring underneath was a live mass of squirming brownish-black bugs. He dropped it again with a shudder. I almost screamed.

"Want to leave now?" asked Niall.

"Oh, yeah." It wasn't just the bugs that made me want to leave. I was still stressed from the whole thing with the beer cans, the bikers. All the new and hostile people in the audience. I needed to decompress after all that, and a room in The Calgarian just didn't seem like the place to do it.

Back home, we made love and talked in my bed for hours with no bugs in sight. Niall seemed so different from the last time we'd been together, a couple of weeks before. He'd shown up late one night, unannounced. He'd been out drinking with

Jason and just had to see me, he said. Of course I let him in, of course we got into bed. He was distant after, quiet. I wanted to know how he got the cut on his lip, and finally got out of him that he and Jason had been involved in some kind of fight. He wouldn't say anything else about it and left soon after, leaving me feeling messed up as usual. But this night he was friendly, warm, affectionate. I never knew which Niall he'd be when I saw him.

He pulled me close and lit two cigarettes, like Paul Henreid in *Now, Voyager*. What a romantic guy.

"So I'm sending out applications to universities. My dad's really getting on my case. He wants me to get into school again," he said.

"I would have thought for sure you'd go to ACA. I've always wondered why you haven't."

"I've thought about it, lots. Sent away for the entrance kit and all that. But I'm not sure art school is the right thing."

"It's different for me. I know what I want, it's just..." I grappled for the words, thought of saying 'you' and decided against it. "...circumstance that gets in the way."

"What do you want? I mean besides going to university and becoming a writer, I know you want to do that."

"Besides that? Do I have to tell you?"

"You want me? But you have me right here right now, don't you?"

"I do, for the moment. That's what gets me. Anyway, it's different for you. You've got the whole world in your lap, you can do whatever you want."

His eyes glittered as he smiled or grimaced; I couldn't tell which. "You think I've got it made, don't you? That because my family has money, life is just one big party for me."

"I don't think that at all. I just think you've got a lot more opportunities than, say, someone like me, who has no money and no connections."

"I guess that's true. I'm not worried about you, though. Anybody who could face up to a room full of angry punk rockers in a wet T-shirt, I'm sure you'll be fine."

"Yeah, as long as I have a bunch of Hell's Angels standing in front of me. And you hovering around somewhere near the back." He smiled the slow, gentle smile that turned my spine to jelly as he located his jeans on the floor and fumbled around in the pockets. "Let's smoke this joint and get dressed and go watch the sun rise. I ought to stop boring you with my stupid worries."

"You could never bore me," I said.

He took a long hit and passed it to me, blew out the smoke slowly before he answered. "That's what I like about you. You're nice."

I coughed a little as I exhaled a lungful of pungent smoke. "That's just my problem. I'm terminally nice. I mean, what do I have to do to be bad? I play in a rock band, I drink, smoke drugs, swear like a sailor, stay up all night and have sex with you whenever I can. And I'm still a nice girl."

He gave me a squeeze. "It's not such a bad thing, you know."

I got dressed and we went downstairs to sit on the front porch. Niall put his arm around me, the sky started to glow orange. The future was shifting in front of me, I realized. He was leaving town. I wasn't going back to school in the fall like I'd planned to. Nothing seemed to be working out the way I thought it would.

12. September 1982

A month later I recalled the night of the DOA gig with mixed feelings as I waited for the bus outside Eaton's after work, the cold wind biting through my jacket. The day had gone by in a heartbeat, throngs of Saturday shoppers a blur. I'd wandered up and down the Eighth Avenue Mall on my lunch hour, felt too sick and distracted to eat or read or do anything but smoke.

A familiar voice at my side broke my daze. "Kate?"

"Dave. How are you?" Niall's brother always looked so together, so relaxed and confident, like someone who knew what he was doing. He wore jeans and a grey sweater, hair neatly trimmed. Much as I liked him, though, I really didn't want to talk to him right then.

"I'm fine. And you?"

"I'm okay."

"Listen, you look cold. Can I give you a ride home?" I must have looked worse than I thought.

We drove down Twelfth Avenue to my place. Dave's car was another Gordon Graham cast-off, a white nineteen-sixties Mercedes sedan.

"Something bothering you?" he wanted to know.

"I'm having a bad day."

"I kind of figured that. This wouldn't happen to have anything to do with my brother, would it?"

Of course it does. It always does. "I got laid off today."

"That sucks."

"Yeah, tell me about it."

"You'll get another job. I'd hire you in a minute."

"Gee, thanks, Dave. I don't know, though. I hear things are bad out there."

"You're sure that's all? You looked miserable at the bus stop."

I considered for a second. "I guess I'm tired. I'll crash for a while when I get home."

He disregarded this. "Why do you let Niall treat you the way he does?"

"I don't know. I guess I'm just a fucking idiot. I guess I'd rather take what I can get from him than see someone else."

"You mean have a real relationship with someone else."

"Yeah. I know you're right. I know he's self-centered. But I always think I see more to him than that. Sometimes little pieces of what he really is show through." Deep down, I thought, I know he's like you. "I'm a lost cause. Someone ought to just take me out behind the barn and shoot me...this is it, right here." The pink and yellow paint on our place had faded and peeled even more. Patches of weathered silver wood showed through around all the edges and one of the front steps had rotted through in the middle.

"Nice place, Old Yeller."

64

"Do you have time to come in for a minute?"

"I'm sorry, I've got to go. I just wanted to make sure you were okay. Someone should look out for you."

He made it sound like I was infirm or something. "I do all right most of the time. Thanks for the ride."

"Take care of yourself." This wasn't the first time I found myself wondering why I didn't have the sense to love Dave, instead. But I thought of Niall's eyes and knew it could never happen. Nobody else was home, to my relief. In recent months, we'd had a steady stream of guests, visitors, parties. Although I was as guilty as anybody else of inviting people over, it got to me sometimes. Often, finding peace or even privacy was difficult. I lay on the couch, flipping through a magazine. I must have fallen asleep, because the next thing I knew, I was answering the doorbell.

"Can I come in?" Niall asked.

"Yeah. Sorry, I was asleep."

"I could come back later."

"No. Come in."

"Dave said he thought you needed someone to talk to. Me, specifically."

"Yeah?" My mouth felt like sand. For a second, I was angry. Where did Dave get off thinking there was something wrong with me, anyway? Smart-ass. Who asked him? He happened to be right, which didn't make me feel any better.

"I think I might be pregnant." After I let out a breath, I looked at him. His face looked unchanged mostly, except that his lips turned white.

"Are you sure?"

"No. I go to the doctor on Monday."

He pulled me close. "So how late are you?"

"Two weeks. I mean, it doesn't necessarily mean anything. But I'm freaking out, just the same."

"Sure. I can see it. I'm freaking out. So if you are, what'll you do?"

"I don't know. I don't think I could get rid of it. I just couldn't. But let's take it one step at a time. First, I'll have the test on Monday."

"How long does it take for the results to come back?"

"I don't know. A few days, I guess." He *was* freaking out. His fingers dug into the flesh of my shoulder like he was holding on for dear life. "Oh, yeah," I continued. "And I got laid off today."

"You're kidding."

"Nope. Today was my last day. So now I'm a pregnant welfare bum, single mom commie pervert punk rocker, or something."

"Man. You are having a bad day. Why didn't you tell me before?"

"I don't know. I kept hoping you'd call me."

He squirmed, like he'd been caught doing something. "Sorry. I didn't know."

"You could have called me, anyway," I suggested.

He sighed. "Listen. Whatever happens, it'll be okay. We'll work something out. In the meantime, I'll stay with you tonight, if that's all right."

"I'd like that. But you know what? I really don't feel like going to bed."

"Me neither. Let's get a pizza instead." Pizza instead of sex—a precedent that, years later, I would regret setting.

When my doctor's office called on Thursday, I felt like my sentence had been commuted. Niall and I walked downtown to The Long Bar that evening, where Clare had got us another booking. I wasn't real happy about it, but at least this time we were supposed to headline. Our little gig with DOA, comical as the whole thing turned out to be, did that for us: we were now headliners. I didn't think we'd ever want to play The Long Bar again after The Suicide Doors incident, but I guessed as headliners we'd be in control. A few months earlier Clare got us a week-long gig there opening for The Suicide Doors, a hardcore outfit. She'd accept any booking, figured the more exposure we got, the better. They had the torn shirts and the dog collars and all that shit. But when it came time for us to get paid, they stiffed us big time. The deal was supposed to be 30% of the door for us, and then they tried to pay us in beer. We made a scene in front of the crowd and the offer changed to a hundred dollars, and after a loud argument we finally got $300 out of them. I didn't feel so bad about getting only $75 each for a week's work after the bartender confided that The Suicide Doors had such a hefty bar tab they might walk away owing money. Still, the whole thing left a bad taste in my mouth and I became more cynical about the so-called alternative scene. Alternative to what, I wondered?

Near the end of our first set a brawl broke out on the dance floor. I didn't think too much of it until I realized I hadn't seen Niall around for a while. I couldn't tell how many guys were involved, it looked like five or six. Jason was in the middle of it. I couldn't see Niall anywhere. The bouncers broke up the fight and threw out all the offending parties, including Jason. We finished the song and I followed him outside.

"Jason, are you okay?"

The streetlights turned the oozing cut under his eye a dark purple. He stood and rubbed his jaw, seemed a bit out of it. "I'm fine. Have you seen Niall?"

"No. I was going to ask you the same thing."

"Look, they won't let me back in there, but I need to talk to him. Would you mind looking for him?" As if I would have done anything else.

I'd almost given up when I finally found him in a corridor near the back door, sitting on a crate, head in his hands. The coward, I thought. His friend gets pounded, and he's hiding.

"Niall," I began, about to tell him off. He looked up at me, smiling a little, mouth dripping red.

"Steel-toed boots," he explained through the marbles in his mouth.

"Jesus!" I got some paper towels out of the can, slowed the flow. "How do you feel?"

"A couple of teeth feel loose. Where's Jason?"

"He got kicked out. He's outside, says he needs to talk to you. What the hell happened?"

He stood up a little unsteadily. "Come on, let's get out of here. I don't know what happened. Jason and I went out in the alley for a puff, and when we get back these guys start beating the shit out of us."

Jude and the gals stared at us as we walked through the bar, up the stairs and out onto the Eighth Avenue Mall where

Jason sat on a bench and smoked a Camel, looking remarkably calm for someone who'd just had the shit beaten out of him. "How did you make out?" he asked Niall.

"I'm a little fucked. They got my head a few times."

Jason stood. "Come on, then. I'll take you to the hospital."

Niall turned to me. "You don't need to sit in Emergency all night. I'll call you tomorrow."

"I don't mind waiting."

"But you've got another set to finish. Don't worry, I'll be fine."

"I'll take care of him," Jason said.

I watched them walk down the mall to Jason's car. I felt outraged, terrified, sick at his pain. And confused. I couldn't understand what had just happened, I couldn't understand why he didn't want me to come with him. I couldn't understand anything right at that moment.

The doorbell rang as I lay on my bed a week later. I heard Wendy walk to the door, open it. I tried to keep my breath shallow, strained to listen, not moving a muscle so the rustle of the bedclothes wouldn't drown out his voice. I didn't even swallow.

I'd resolved not to see him again. I'd also resolved to stop thinking about him, with the result that I spent a lot of time thinking about how I wasn't thinking about him. But I had to move on, I told myself. Clare and Jude had said it enough times that I started to believe it, perhaps. Intellectually, I had known it for a long time, just like intellectually I knew I ought to quit smoking. But this night I decided to ask Wendy to tell him I was out. I couldn't make out what they said, I just heard his deeper voice, then her higher one. I heard his muffled voice coming up through the floor, couldn't make out what he said, and felt my body pull itself off the bed. I had to hang on to the mattress frame and sink my teeth into my lower lip so I wouldn't rush down before he left. I knew I'd only have to show myself downstairs and soon we'd be up here. I tried to forget the feel of his warmth, about breathing him in, tasting the slight salt of his flesh. One last time, one last time. Once more couldn't matter, couldn't make any difference, now.

Before I even understood that I'd made up my mind, I made it halfway down the stairs. Then I hesitated and hid in the shadows of the stairwell. I waited. I couldn't make a fool of Wendy. Finally, she closed the door and I came silently the rest of the way down. She saw me and gave me the thumbs up, but before she could speak, I ran past her through the kitchen, out the back door, through the yard and into the alley. Then I cut through the empty lot and popped out onto the sidewalk, as if I'd been out for a stroll, just as he started up his car.

"Hello," he said.

What to say, what to say. I was still angry about last time I'd seen him, about everything. And yet here I was. "Hello yourself. How are your teeth?"

"Better now. I didn't lose any."

"That's good. You're otherwise okay, no concussion or anything like that?"

"Nope. I was kind of tired for a day or two, but I feel a lot better now."

"Good. So what brings you around here?"

"Just came to see what you were up to."

I shrugged. "Want to come in?"

Wendy only shook her head when we came back in. I wanted to tell her how ashamed I was, how useless and stupid and weak I felt. But I couldn't. I couldn't even look her in the eye.

13. December 1982

I'd spent Christmas of 1981 with Jude's family. The Morrisons were good people, very kind to me, but they weren't my family. I wasn't sure if that was good or bad, actually. In one way I was relieved to be away from Carmen and Dad. Tensions always ran high around the Brandt household during the festive season, the highlight being the annual

Christmas Eve Fight, and me with a ringside seat. Many times I spent the holidays relaying season's greetings from one parent to another. *Tell him I think he's a drunken loser. You tell your mother she's being unreasonable. Tell him I said everything I'm going to say to him last week.* Of course, I had some good memories, too, mostly of Christmases when I was little, when they hadn't started drinking so much yet. And I always still hoped that maybe it would get better, maybe this would be the year they wouldn't fight. Even so, I missed them at Christmas, and I decided to give Carmen a call. I hadn't talked to her since I moved out the summer before.

"Hello, Carmen."

"Kate, is that you?"

"Yes, it is. How are you?"

"I'm fine. Your father's fine. Are you all right?"

"I'm fine, too."

"I just wondered what brought this on. I thought you might be in some kind of trouble."

I sighed. Why couldn't she be nice for once? "No, everything is fine. I just thought since it's Christmas I might come over."

"I guess we could do that. It would be nice to see you again."

"I'd like to see you and Dad, too."

"Well, when would you like to come over? Christmas Eve? Christmas Day?"

"Um, how about Christmas Day? In the afternoon sometime?" Maybe they'd have the fight out of the way by then.

"Sure. I hope you'll stay for dinner, too."

"Thanks, I will."

When I got off the phone I felt pretty good about the way the call had gone. While Carmen hadn't sounded exactly thrilled that I had called, at least she was mostly agreeable. It occurred to me then that maybe she had felt as bad and as awkward as I had all the time we hadn't spoken. Maybe it wasn't that she didn't want to make the first move, maybe she just didn't know how.

Once I got that settled, I could go back to feeling bad about Niall. He'd been over a week earlier, things had seemed

70

fine, we'd had wonderful, passionate sex. Then two nights later at a party I went to with Jude and Barb, he spent almost the entire time talking to a girl he'd brought. I'd never seen her before, a small, round-faced girl with dark brown hair in a pixie cut. No-one seemed to know her.

"Hey, who's the fat-assed little troll Niall's with?" asked Barb.

"Damned if I know. Never saw her before. Any of that wine left?"

I spent most of the time in a corner of the kitchen, drinking far too much. The Talking Heads played loud and they bored me senseless. I could feel the music pound up from the floor through my feet. It got so loud that we couldn't talk. The other people in the kitchen danced. I watched Niall in the living-room talk to Miss X. He seemed to be enjoying himself.

Finally, he sought me out, just as Jude and I were about to leave. He smiled and slid his arm around me. "What are you hiding out here for?"

I slithered out of his grasp. "Who wants to know?"

He seemed surprised. "What's the matter?"

"Nothing. We were just leaving." I put on my black fun fur coat and tried to step by him.

"But I haven't even had a chance to wish you a Merry Christmas."

"Well, I guess if you'd been able to pry yourself away from your little friend, there, you might have been able to do it. I've been here all night, you know."

"Her name is Karen."

"Karen, is it? Swell. Well, Merry fucking Christmas, Niall. I've got to go now."

He took hold of my arm, tried to pull me close. I jerked my arm away.

"Merry Christmas, Kate."

John Petersen, ex-Sister, threw a Year's Eve Party and I knew Niall would be there. I changed my plans hundreds of times. I wouldn't go. I'd go, and bring a man. I finally decided to go looking like a million dollars, and let this Karen person wilt in my glorious presence. I wore a deep red brocade nineteen-fifties dress with a plunging neckline and fringed hem. I should almost have been sewn into it. I decided to bring a stitch ripper in case I got lucky.

Niall wasn't there when we arrived at 9.30. He still hadn't shown at 10.30, and by 11.00, I became officially despondent. He and Karen were probably dancing some romantic troll dance in the Palliser ballroom, linking their arms for a sip of champagne. Maybe he was drinking it out of her little troll slipper, the bastard. Then, at a quarter to midnight, he appeared. He spotted me from across the room, made his way over.

"Hello," he said quietly. He smelled of liquor, looked like maybe he'd caught a snooze under a bridge or something.

"Hello." I couldn't bring myself to smile at him, although I was relieved he'd come alone this time.

"You look wonderful." I could almost feel his eyes move up and down my body.

I cleared my throat. "Thank you." I did not ask where he'd been, lit my four-hundredth cigarette of the night.

"I didn't really feel much like partying tonight. I wasn't going to come. Jason and I were hanging out at CJSW. I'm glad I did, now. I'm glad you're here."

I looked up at him. Oh, Christ, there was no hope for me. I melted into a big, stupid puddle. "Me, too." What a maroon.

"I wanted to talk to you last time, but you didn't seem very interested. I think you got the wrong idea about me and Karen."

"Did I?"

"She's the daughter of one of my dad's clients. I took her out as a favour."

I relaxed a little. "You seemed to enjoy talking to her."

Did he blush? He looked at his watch, started to open the bottle of champagne he brought. "Could you dig up some glasses? She's a nice enough girl. And I had to talk to her, she didn't know anybody else. She and I aren't an item, you know."

The countdown started. He filled two coffee mugs, the only clean vessels I could find, with champagne from the

Graham wine cellar. Then he pulled me up for a kiss.

"Happy 1983, Kate," he said when we released ourselves.

"Happy New Year."

Things would be okay, I told myself. They'd be like they always were, I knew: okay, sort of. He'd come over after the party, stay tangled in my arms until noon or so the next day. And then I might not see him again for weeks. Or he might be over the next night. But I wanted more, I wanted to possess him the way he'd possessed me all this time. Still, right then he was with me. I didn't want to think about the rest of it. I'd think about that tomorrow.

We left the party earlier than Jude and the others, got back to the house around 1.30. We sat on the couch, lit up a reefer.

"I felt shitty all week, Kate. I knew you were mad, hurt. I didn't want you to feel like that, but I didn't know what to do."

"You could have called me."

"But you were mad. What if you had hung up?"

"Niall. Would I hang up on you?"

"Maybe."

"Well, maybe. You know it wouldn't mean anything, though. Think about it—why was I mad in the first place? Because I love you."

He held me closer for a moment then pulled back, and stroked my hair. "I—"

He stopped. "What?" I asked.

"I'm lucky I have you."

What were you really going to say? I thought about asking. But I didn't, there was no point. He'd never say it in a million years.

14. August 1983

I woke to find Niall pulling the blankets up around me. It was early and there was always a damp chill in the sunroom.

"You can't sleep in here again this winter. You almost died of pneumonia last year," he told me.

How could I still be amazed to find him beside me, mornings? Sometimes I woke before he did, and I'd just watch him sleep, drink him in. Maybe if I did it long enough I could suck in his soul or something. That's probably what he thought would happen. Or he'd wake up and all of a sudden we'd be married. Even though I told him I didn't ever want to marry, I don't think he believed me. Now he propped himself up on one elbow, twirled his index finger in my hair and I could lie there and watch him forever. My thrift store curtains fit pretty well, they were cool old ivory lace sheers. I loved that room, and I didn't care how cold it got.

"To listen to you, anybody would think you cared about me."

"I do care about you."

I raised my eyebrows, reached over to the crate beside the mattress for a smoke. "Really?"

"You know I do. I'm just not in love with you, that's all."

"That's all, eh? You make it sound so trivial."

I couldn't say what I really wanted to. How could I tell him that the only time I felt alive was when he was beside me? Or that I thought of him the second I woke up in the morning, every day, that my pulse still raced and my mouth got dry every time I saw him? He didn't want to hear all that. But I couldn't help that it was true.

He ignored the direction the conversation took. He was good at that. "I've been accepted at York. I'm leaving soon."

"You just found this out?"

"No. But I wasn't sure at first that I wanted to go. And then I wasn't sure how to tell you."

"Oh. So when do you leave?"

"Two weeks."

I took a deep breath, let it out again slowly. "It's in Toronto, right?"

He nodded. Toronto. Only a few thousand miles from Calgary. What a hell of a way to start a morning.

"ACA has one of the best programs in North America, you know. You'd be much better off there."

"I know. But I'm not going to York to take art. I mean, I'll take some arts courses, I guess. But I'll get a communications degree, then go to law school."

He sounded pretty decided. I thought about arguing, but resistance seemed useless. "Are you happy about it?"

"Sure, I guess."

"You don't sound very excited."

"My parents are excited, and they're paying for it. It's a good school. Dad did law at Osgoode Hall and he has his heart set on me doing the same. The Grahams have been taking law there since the eighteen-eighties."

"What do *you* have your heart set on?"

He smiled and pushed the lock of hair he'd been playing with behind my ear. "I don't know. You ask the strangest questions sometimes."

"What's so strange? You must have some idea of what you'd like to do."

"I'm not sure it matters. Anyway, right now, that's what I'm doing."

I persisted. "You have talent. You know you do. You should follow your heart, like Dave is."

"I can't be like him. I can't be like you, either. I can't live through my heart instead of my head." Me, I couldn't imagine even having a choice in the matter.

On Niall's last night in Calgary, John threw a party in his honour at his house in Erlton, a stone's throw from Victoria Park. John lived in a two-storey, three-bedroom house with three other guys, all in various bands and in various states of employment or unemployment. Old tires and plastic milk crates decorated their living-room. People constantly came and went and played music in the basement. At John's, it was hard to tell a party from the usual state of affairs. I arrived about 10.00. Not too many people had arrived yet, but John emerged from the basement shortly after I arrived and threw his arms around me.

"Welcome. I'm happy you could make it," he grinned, rye on his breath. I couldn't help but notice he looked good, green eyes full of mischief. Or rye, anyway. "And might I add that you look divine tonight. The guest of honour hasn't arrived yet, but I'm glad you're here to give him the old shove-off with me."

Not here yet? Where is he? There's so little time left. "I didn't wear this for your benefit, John," I told him. I removed his arm from my shoulder and smoothed down the burgundy velvet of my dress where his hand had been. Then Niall arrived. The family had a big dinner for him and Dave and he couldn't have got away any sooner, he said.

Maggie and Derek hung out in the kitchen. She asked me how I was, and I said okay.

"You're lying. I know you're not okay. Why don't you go and chase him down?"

"I can't chase him down. He's leaving."

"No, I mean follow him out there. What's stopping you?"

"I have no money, for one thing." I also had no courage. Following him would require courage, if not complete foolhardiness. "What could be crazier than moving to a city thousands of miles away where I know no-one, following someone who doesn't want me around? Oh, yeah, and with no money."

"You could hitchhike."

"I guess I could do that. I'll have to see how desperate I get."

She just shrugged. She knew as well as I did that I'd thought about it. The whole idea didn't make much sense, but I kept it in reserve anyway.

About 12.30 I leaned up against Niall's car and waited for him. I wanted to be out of there, wanted to have him to myself, but he was saying goodbyes to old friends.

We'd arranged earlier that he'd come home with me and I was glad the house was empty when we finally got there. Up in my room we made love slowly, almost silently. I couldn't help feeling miserable even with him inside me, his mouth on mine, knowing that this would be the last time. Probably the last time ever.

All too soon we shared a cigarette, then he started to dress.

"You can't go already," I whispered, defeated. Of course he was going. Resistance is useless.

"I have to. Dave and I have to get up at 6.30, gotta be on

the road by 7.30. We're packed already, all we have to do is get up and go. But it's almost 3.00 now." He dressed, went to the bathroom. I threw on my big old white terry bathrobe and stared out the window, wondered what our final words might be.

"Aren't you going to come down and say goodbye?"

Silently, I followed him. Things already started to blur. I tried not to cry. Did I want my last words to him to be unintelligible? I needed to say something memorable, witty, pithy. Where's that damned *Portable Dorothy Parker* when you need it, eh?

We stood under the huge old poplar in the front yard whose leaves already started to turn yellow. He leaned against the trunk, pulled me close. I managed to smile. He brushed a fallen leaf from my shoulder.

"I guess this is goodbye," he said finally.

"Oh, Niall," I whispered. Say, that was witty. I found I couldn't say anything else. I buried my face in his chest. A moment later he lifted my face.

"Don't cry," he told me. Hey, why didn't I think of that? I couldn't hold back then. He rubbed my shoulders and I eventually calmed down to the point where I could speak.

"I'm sorry," I told him, as I blew my nose in a Kleenex I found in my pocket. Was he looking around, up and down the street to see if anyone else saw us, at a time like this? He was, the bastard.

"Don't be sorry. I didn't know you still felt this way. Do you still need me this much?"

"Of course I do. Do you think I stopped loving you just because you don't love me?"

He shrugged. "Most people would."

"I don't know what I'm going to do. I feel like I might just die."

He stroked my hair. The streetlight softly lit his. He looked wonderful. "You won't die. You'll be glad this day came, soon. You'll be better off without me around, you'll start seeing other guys. You'll see. You'll forget me in six months."

"How can you think I would forget you?"

77

"I'm kidding. I know you well enough by now." He gave me his trademark brotherly squeeze. "It'll be good for both of us."

"Is that why you're going to York? To get away from me?"

"Of course not. You know why I'm going. It just happens that…this will be good. You need to see other people, and so do I. John's dying to go out with you."

"I don't want to see John. I don't want to see anyone else," I whispered. Maybe he could kick me in the stomach, too.

He kissed me. "I've got to go. Goodbye, Kate," he said, and pulled away from my arms. I wanted to affix myself to him so that he'd be forced to drive home with me stuck to him, and then drive out to Toronto like that. Now was the time to say that devastatingly witty something for him to remember me by. But, like those dreams I had where I wanted to scream and no sound would come out of my mouth, I was temporarily mute.

"Goodbye, Niall," I finally blurted out as he closed the car door. He waved as he pulled away, I waved back to the blurry car. "I love you," I added pointlessly.

He was gone. I sat under the tree and cried. I got cold, then I got thirsty. But grief rooted me to the ground. I felt hollowed out, unable to do anything but cry. Thankfully, after a time something won out over my grief: my nicotine addiction. My cigarettes, I knew, were in my bedroom and eventually I had to go in. As I lit one I caught a glimpse of myself in the mirror in the bathroom (*please talk free*) and for just a second, my smeared makeup, messy hair, bathrobe and cigarette all came together to convince me that it was Carmen I saw. But then she disappeared and it was just me again.

By the time Jude came into the kitchen next morning, I had dressed and started drinking coffee. I mean, I'd already been out for more smokes, don't you know?

"Morning. How are you?" she asked.

"I'm here."

She poured herself a mug of coffee, topped off mine. She found her cigarettes in the pocket of her robe and sat down at the table with me.

"Want a smoke?"

"Okay. Thanks. I love smokes."

She lit both our cigarettes, took a long drag, let the smoke out slowly and silently. "You know it's good that he's gone, don't you?"

"That's what he said."

"He was right. You couldn't go on like that, living on strands of hope that you'd hang on to like a drowning woman every time he had a drunken moment of weakness and let some of his feelings slip out. You know he's a heartless bastard. And I'm not just saying that."

I bit at the ragged edge of a fingernail. I always bit my nails down as far as I could without pain. Well, without too much pain. I knew where the threshold was, knew just how far I could bite before I hit it. "I know. Don't you think I know he can be heartless? I also know he can be kind and affectionate. And maybe you wouldn't believe it, but he can be caring. Someone who's really heartless couldn't be all those things."

"Maybe not. Although I'm betting he was only like that when he wanted to get laid."

"Not true. You don't know him like I do."

"Okay, I'm sorry. I shouldn't slag the recently departed. And I don't want you to cry. I can just imagine how much you've been crying. You're probably getting dehydrated."

"The funny thing is, it seems like I used to feel better when I had a good cry. Now it doesn't make any difference. I cry and cry, and I still feel like shit, but I can't stop. And you know what I just realized? I don't have a thing to remind me of him. Not a picture, not a sweater or anything like that."

"You've got pictures in your yearbooks. And you almost had his baby. Doesn't that count for something?"

The doorbell rang, bringing a timely end to what was becoming, in my opinion, a very bad conversation. Clare joined us for a coffee while we waited for Barb to arrive and for Wendy to get up.

"You look wiped, Kate. Maybe we shouldn't practice today," she suggested.

"I'll be okay."

Clare put her hand over mine. "This is for the best."

"That's what everybody keeps saying. I feel like if I was a

dog, they'd have put me to sleep long ago."

"We just didn't think of it," Jude reassured me.

Clare glared at her. "Ignore her. I wanted to save this little bit of news until everyone else got here. Well, I don't know if I would have waited for Wendy. Anyway, maybe it'll cheer you up. Remember I took our demo tape and those photos Riva did to a management company a while back?"

"Sure, I remember. I looked like a real ratbag in those photos. Troy and that other dude came to see us at The National that night and then nothing ever happened. I thought they weren't interested."

"You did not look like a ratbag. I thought they weren't interested, too. But we were wrong. Troy called last night and they've made us an offer. We have an opportunity to go work in Tuktoyaktuk for a year."

"Tuktoyaktuk? In the Northwest Territories?"

Clare smiled expectantly. "That's right."

I looked blankly at her. I always rained on her little parades. "Why would we want to do that?"

"Why? Because it would be a solid year of playing in front of an audience, and getting paid well for it. Think how much better we'd get. Like the Beatles in Hamburg kind of thing. The hotel, The Beaufort Inn I think Troy said, would pay us $6000 a month. And free accommodation and meals. It would start November 1st. How can we say no?"

I thought about this for a minute. Before, there would have been no way I would have considered such a thing. But there was nothing to keep me in Calgary now.

"Sure, let's do it. Sounds better than the Foreign Legion."

15. October 1983

We flew to Edmonton one afternoon and stayed overnight so we could take the first flight to Inuvik, and after that we'd get a smaller plane to Tuktoyaktuk. I knew that Tuktoyaktuk was a long way from Calgary, almost 3700 km away. But I didn't really comprehend how far north of Edmonton we'd have to go, had no idea until then how far north this country stretches. The flight from Edmonton to Inuvik took five hours. It was a clear day, pretty good weather for October. And what we could see out the window was mostly trees; we were disappearing into trees, it felt like. Trees, trees, lakes, rivers, trees. As we got closer to Inuvik the trees got sparser, pretty soon there weren't any more. Then it was bare tundra dotted with lakes and ponds.

In Inuvik we caught our flight to Tuktoyaktuk, which would take about 45 minutes. The plane was a ten-seater Cessna, didn't look much bigger than my dad's Olds 88. I couldn't help myself; once we were in the air I said, "Buddy Holly." Carmen had brought him up when I told her about the trip, hoping to dissuade me from going.

"Let's not think about him right now," said Clare.

"Who's Buddy Holly?" asked Wendy.

"C'mon," I said. "Buddy Holly and The Crickets? *Peggy Sue? That'll Be the Day?*"

"Never heard of him," Wendy said.

"He was a pretty influential early rocker from Texas," said Clare. "He and Ritchie Valens and The Big Bopper died in a plane crash on a tour."

"Yeah, but he was older than us," I said. "He was 22."

The pilot pointed out the town of Tuktoyaktuk to us as we approached, the northernmost community on the Canadian mainland, he said. It looked like a few streets with houses and buildings scattered along them, spread out on a narrow spit that curled into Kugmalit Bay. Soon, the pilot said, the whole spit would be surrounded with ice and stay that way until the spring thaw.

The air terminal on the outskirts of Tuktoyaktuk was tiny, even smaller than the one in Inuvik. We got out of the plane and the pilot helped us unload our equipment right onto the runway. Then we caught a cab to The Beaufort Inn, only a few minutes down the main road.

November 27, 1983

Dear Jude:
Sorry it's taken me so long to write. This place is nuts. We haven't even been here a month yet and already it seems like years. It is fucking cold up here! Makes Calgary look almost tropical. Tuktoyaktuk, or Tuk, as the locals call it, is the base for oil exploration in the Beaufort Sea, so there are lots of oil and gas workers up here (trying not to refer to them as 'rig pigs' although it's apt in many cases). So, I have good news, bad news and weird news.

The good news: Never imagined making this kind of money before, especially playing music. Beats the hell out of being paid in beer. And the hotel pays for our room and meals. And drinks! My only expense so far has been smokes. Another good thing is we're getting loads of practice in, as you can well imagine. Already we're so much tighter, and we've got almost another whole set ready. I wish you could hear us. I'll send a tape once I get my shit together.

The bad news: It's fucking cold up here! Thank God they sell cigarettes here at the hotel. I haven't been inside all the time, but the place is small, it's flat as Saskatchewan and there isn't much to do. I love the sea, so sometimes we walk along the inner harbour, but there isn't much to look at and the wind coming off the water is cold as hell. Other bad news: I can see how too much togetherness could be bad for us. We are getting better, but I also think we're getting sick of each other. A Catch-22 experienced by many bands, no doubt: you just start to get good and by that time you can't stand the sight of each other. Clare is getting on my nerves. The only thing that keeps me from killing her is that she's spending a lot of time with her new boyfriend, Lou, the bartender. Wendy is also making me crazy, probably more than anyone else because we're sharing a room. Debbie and I are doing okay so far, but she's been with us, what, a couple of months? The thing is, I was used to Barb's style of playing. Debbie is throwing me because her bass lines are so much more complicated and tuneful than Barb's. Which reminds me, have you heard from her? I couldn't believe it when she told us two weeks before we left for Tuk that she was going to Toronto and joining that thrash band, PMS. I'm still pissed off at her. Oh, well. I seem to be pissed off at almost everybody these days. Maybe I should get outside more, come to think of it. Actually, I don't spend all of my time with the gals, because of my weird news. There's a new man in my life.

It felt really weird to write that, to think it even. But it's true. You remember James, the dark-haired lead guitarist with Dogfaced Boy? We're opening for them and, well, things just happened. He's unbelievable. He's nearly driven Niall out of my mind. He's got quite an imagination, and quite a repertoire. Ahem. I suspect that there is a direct relationship between these well-developed abilities and the number of, shall we say, opportunities he's had to hone them. Oh, well. I won't think about that right now.

That reminds me, have you seen John around at all? I feel bad about how things didn't work out between us. I could only think about Niall every time he kissed me. It was too soon, I guess.

Anyway, that's life here at The Beaufort Inn. Work, play, love, hate, eating, drinking, smoking and everything else in between. The hotel is just a little universe unto itself. You ought to come visit our galaxy sometime. We miss you, of course, me most of all.

Love,
Kate

That was a long winter, all right. Soon I lost track of time. Didn't know or care what day of the week it was because it just didn't matter, and every day was exactly like the other. We'd play two sets a night, one at 8.30 and one at 10.30, head for bed around 3.30 or 4.00, sleep until 11.00 or so, rehearse in the afternoon. We worked every night except for Christmas, and we had the same crowd every night, always almost all men. Hard-working, hard-drinking men. Things improved a little once the summer came along. We got out more then. There still wasn't much to do, but at least we didn't freeze our asses off every time we walked along the shore. It was still cold, though not much colder than Calgary in the summer, come to think of it. And Tuk had a lot more mosquitoes. In the summer it was light most of the time. Even when it did get dark briefly, between about 11 PM and 2 AM, it was really just dim.

Jude came for a two-week visit in June. I was so glad to see her. I don't think I realized how homesick I felt until she came. She hung out and watched us practice, we went for walks during the day. She caught me up on all the local news—who was in what band, who was sleeping with who. She loved taking history at the University, had a condo up near the campus. She told me she couldn't wait until I saw it.

"I'd love to see it," I said. "I'd love to go home. I'd love to go to The National with you and quaff once more that disgusting sour pee-yellow draft, the amazing beverage which looks and tastes much the same coming in and going out. Actually, they have it here, too, but it's just not the same, you know?"

"Come on. That stuff is the same everywhere."

"I don't believe it."

I hated to tell her about James. So much for healing my poor battered and broken heart. I should have known that he would turn out to be a gigantic asshole. I should have known—no, I did know—that a guy with that kind of technique has been with more than a few women, and I certainly wouldn't be the last. Looking back, I doubted that I was even exclusive at the time. So why oh why did I allow it to continue? Because he was just so damned good, and I was on the rebound in a major way.

"Did you love him?" she asked.

"I don't know. I miss him, almost as much as Dogfaced Boy does. He left town two weeks ago, never even said goodbye. I sure can pick 'em, no?"

On the bright side, things amongst us women weren't too bad. I felt, at least at that moment, that there was hope for us. I liked some of the new covers we'd added to our roster, like T. Rex's *Rock On*, Memphis Minnie's *Black Cat Blues* and The Poppees' *Jealousy*. And fending off the drunks every night gave us a real sense of solidarity. We wished they'd set up some barbed wire around the tiny square of scuffed linoleum that served as a stage, maybe outfit us with some sten guns. One guy came to the show every night, and yelled, "Blondie! I'll make it hard for you in five minutes!" Great.

It seemed like some of these fellas had difficulty in distinguishing musicians from prostitutes, if you can imagine that. Not that prostitutes were hard to find. The huge number of oil and gas workers meant a huge number of prostitutes. They stood outside the hotel, bored-looking native women mostly.

I couldn't help thinking of Katya. Which of them would be killed like she was, the story a splash in the papers for a few days and then nothing? It made me sad.

When the time came, I hated to see Jude go. I went to the air terminal with her and watched her plane until it was just a little dot in the sky. I wanted so badly to go with her, couldn't stand the idea of five more months of this. In some ways, I felt like we were doing time up there. Sometimes I wanted to just pack up and leave, contract or no. Was it my turn to be commitment-shy now?

In Tuktoyaktuk we made a bit of a change in musical direction. Even before we got up there, our new manager Troy suggested we include a few top 40-type numbers in our set lists. We now had two full 45-minute sets, almost half of them originals. The other half were covers like Hank Williams' *Cold, Cold Heart,* T-Bone Walker's *Stormy Monday* and The Yardbirds' *Still I'm Sad.* Clare and I just told Troy, oh yeah, sure, we'll do some top 40, very soon. I thought Clare was with me, thought she had no intention of doing any such thing. And then she and Wendy ganged up on me at practice one afternoon.

"You want to do *what*?" I asked. I had to sit down at one of the giant round tables in the conference-room where we practised. The big room had lots of chairs, a nice red carpet and ashtrays galore. My kind of room.

"*Queen of Hearts.* You know, that Dave Edmunds song," Clare told me, and handed me the chords and lyrics she'd written out.

"I know the song. But I can't help hearing Juice Newton every time I think of it. Ecch. What brought this on?"

"Well, we did agree to try some top 40 stuff in our set, remember?"

"We didn't exactly agree. I thought that was just lip service."

Wendy stepped in. "You know, I'm sure the audience would appreciate hearing something they're familiar with for a change. I mean, they're normal, working guys. Speaking from a normal person's perspective, I'm sure they find all this

85

Yardbirds, Hank Williams and Buzzcocks stuff a little weird."

"Right. Thank God I know who is the spokesperson for normality in the group, here. Maybe we should do some normal stuff, like a few Joy Division tunes?"

Debbie ignored us, practised her bass scales; she'd got used to us by this time. She kept outside of all this, in a good way. She just did her job, kept out of these little discussions. Her playing was good, not flashy, in the same way her clothes were tasteful, not flashy. Like a good bass player should, she blended into the woodwork. I used to be like that once, I thought. I blended in. Not such a bad way to be.

Clare got angry. "Listen, don't get your shit in a knot here, Kate. We're just trying something different. It won't compromise your artistic integrity to do a song that somebody's actually heard in the last five years."

I gave in. "Okay, fine."

We worked on it for a week, then played *Queen of Hearts* one night. The crowd loved it, of course. I knew they would. I felt like a damned fool singing that song. I fucking hated it. But once the precedent had been set, the top 40 floodgates had opened wide and I had no recourse, as the lone dissenter. Debbie, like Sweden, remained aggravatingly neutral. And now Clare and Wendy went power mad with top 40 tunes. We covered the Go-Go's *Vacation,* Blondie's *The Tide is High,* The Pretenders' *Brass in Pocket,* all those girl-rock tunes I heard on the radio a billion times. Now I had to sing them. I knew this would happen someday. I should have gone to confession long ago. Now it was too late: I was damned.

But Clare took pity on me one night. We were up late, long after we'd finished. The house lights were all off except for the ones at the bar. Lou mixed Clare whiskey sour after whiskey sour, I had a few beers. "I know you hate these new songs. I don't like them myself," she confided. "You've got to just look at this as rehearsal for the big time. I mean, what does it matter if we played a few cheeseball tunes on our way up? When we go to record our first album, none of that stuff will be on it."

But I didn't think I could stand to hang around until that

happened. We ended up being disappointed by the whole experience of playing up there. On the flight up, we felt hyped, we thought this was the start of the big time for us. No more getting paid a hundred dollars, no more getting paid in beer, no more not getting paid at all. As Wendy observed, there are easier ways to make a hundred dollars, easier ways to get fucked. By this time I realized The Beaufort Inn could have been any hotel, anywhere, it didn't matter. I hated living there. We might as well have been in jail. I loved to play music, but if it meant I'd have to live like this for however long it took for us to get to the top of the pops, I didn't think I could do it. It just wasn't what I wanted to do anymore.

But it was more than that, more than not wanting to live in hotels, not wanting to play top 40 garbage. I still loved music, but I couldn't even make the effort to be creative right then. I hadn't written a song in ages, hadn't even helped with one. Maybe it was some kind of spiritual ennui, or something. And having to sing *Queen of Hearts* didn't help. I wanted to go home.

Lou closed down the bar and he and Clare slunk off to his room. I went to the room I shared with Wendy, glad to find her asleep already. I drunkenly removed most of my makeup, put on the flannel pyjamas that I'd taken to wearing since James fucked off, and went to bed. And lay there in the dark, awake. I was the Awake Drunk you always read about in those leaflets, the drunk who's had all the coffee, sitting there looking nervous and bug-eyed. Only it wasn't coffee that kept me awake, it was this damn funk I was in. Deep down, I knew it was same thing it'd always been. James hadn't driven Niall out of my head at all, he'd just distracted me for a while. When Niall was with me I could forget all the frustration, the anger that went along with being in love with him. But it always bubbled there under the surface, that old black angst, and sometimes it didn't take much for it to spill out, especially if I hadn't seen him in a while or if there was something bad going down between us. Then there'd be messy, toxic, evil feelings all over the place (someone get a mop). So now he was gone. And what was happening? I was turning into an asshole, that's what. Like Frank Zappa said: *Ladies, you can be an asshole, too*. I used to be just a part-time one. Now I was sarcastic and angry almost all the time, a full-time asshole who wanted to go home. Or maybe not home, but somewhere else, anywhere else. I wanted to leave.

16. October 1984

On a bright, warm Friday afternoon I soaked for a long time in a bathtub at the downtown Calgary Holiday Inn. My wrinkled toes poked out over the jasmine-scented bubbles, and I thought about the future. It was wide open, so wide open I was terrified into inertia. I felt like I didn't even know who I was, much less what I wanted. I had some money, though. I did have that. Maybe I could just stay right where I was, right in this bathtub. But if I did the money would be all gone in a few months, and even now the water was getting cold.

Once we'd finished out our one-year contract in Tuktoyaktuk, Misclairol ended. Not with a bang, not even a whimper. We just fizzled out. I think by this time we all felt fed up, not just me. Or maybe everybody else was just fed up with me. The long trip home was mostly quiet. There was no more talk of further work together, just a mutual understanding that things were over. I can't say I felt good about that part of it but it was a relief to be back in town. Being back in a city felt great.

Jude had picked us up at the airport and driven us all home, and dropped me off last at my hotel. I'd thought about staying at the Palliser for a night or two but decided I'd better not blow my money too fast. I did have more money than I'd ever had before but still, if I was thinking of university at some point it wouldn't last forever. So the Holiday Inn was good enough for me.

Jude rolled down her window as I took my bags out of the back and put them on the sidewalk in the hotel parking-lot. It really was a beautiful day, like summer, but I was all fucked up from getting up early and the long flight, wasn't in the state of mind to appreciate it. "You can stay with me, you know," she'd said. "Why waste your money on a hotel?"

"I appreciate the offer, Jude. And I may take you up on it later. But right now I need to be alone for a while."

"I would think you'd be sick of hotels by now."

"Yeah, there is that. But I do just need to think for a couple of days."

So that was where I was that afternoon. My band had broken up. Niall was long gone, probably had forgotten all about me the way I should have been forgetting about him. I had no job. I didn't even have any plans, besides a vague one to go back to school at some point. Jude and I did have a plan to go out to dinner that night, which meant I would have to get out of the bathtub eventually and do something besides fret. I could, after all, fret and get ready to go out at the same time, had done so many times before.

The evening continued to be unseasonably warm, although not warm enough that we could eat on a patio. Jude and I did get a table at the big window in the Greek restaurant we went to, so it was almost like being outside. It was funny to be home again after a year and see how everything looked pretty much the same, but different too. Even Jude. She looked the same and different, though I couldn't have told you exactly how the same and how different. She wore jeans and a green sweater, and her hair was longer, dyed more of a chestnut colour now. But it was more than that, something I couldn't put my finger on.

I leaned back in my chair and lit a cigarette after we'd finished eating, felt the retsina do a job on my toes. "It's really good to be back, you know that? The last few weeks had been kind of stressful."

"Were you fighting?"

"Not exactly fighting. We'd sort of done fighting a month or so before and I guess we realized we still had to finish out the contract, so the fighting came to an end. But there was still a lot of hostility. Mostly the unspoken kind."

"That can be worse."

I thought about Dad and Carmen. They did both kinds of hostility, spoken and unspoken. "Yeah, in some ways. I think Clare is right pissed off at me. She'll probably never speak to me again."

"Why? Were you the instigator? Did you break things up?"

"I guess. I don't know. I mean, I was definitely unhappy, but I don't think I was the only one. It seemed more like general rot just set in."

"Either way, I'm sure she'll get over it. Eventually."

"I guess. The band was always her baby, and she's mad that I don't want to be in it anymore."

"Well, you can't change feeling like that, can you? It was time. So will you join another band?"

"Not right now. I don't know what I'm doing at all right now."

"What about going back to school?"

"I was. It's too late for this semester, but I guess I could start in January. I'm not sure if I should do that or if I should go back next fall instead. Either way I'll have to get a job. And find a place to live."

"My place is close to the university, less than a ten minute walk. And I have lots of room. There are two bedrooms. Why don't you stay with me?"

"It's kind of you to offer, but I don't think I could afford the rent at your place."

"There is no rent. My parents bought the place, didn't I tell you that? They figured if I stayed in town and they bought me a condo it would be cheaper than if I went to school out east and they had to pay rent for me out there."

Imagine that. I couldn't, really. "Maybe you did tell me and I just forgot. Wow. No rent. That would be a huge help, not having to worry about that. Are you serious?" The waitress came by and cleared our dishes, poured the rest of the retsina into our glasses.

"Of course I am. I missed you like hell all that time. It'll be good to have you back. And I have this all figured out." Jude smiled.

"Oh, you do?" I wondered for a second what she meant.

90

Still, after all this time, I wondered sometimes if she still felt about me the way she used to.

"Sure. How long are you at your hotel?"

"I'm booked in for two nights."

"Fine. So tomorrow night we go to The National and you can get caught up with people. Then I'll come pick you up on Sunday. On Monday you can come up to the university with me and pick up the forms you need and get all the paperwork shit that's got to happen rolling so you can be ready to start in January. Then you can look for a job after that."

"Wow. You should be a manager or something."

"Yeah, maybe. So what do you think?"

"If it's all right with you, I think it sounds great."

"Excellent. Looking forward to having you around again. By the way, did I tell you I love that dress?"

"Thanks," I smoothed the full chiffon skirt of the black cocktail dress. "I was so excited about eating somewhere besides the Tuk Inn I thought I'd dress up."

"You didn't get it up there, did you?"

"Oh, no. I didn't buy any clothes up there. I bought this just before we left but I never did wear it."

"Well, you look wonderful. It's so good to see you again."

"Thanks. It's good to see you, too. And thanks for getting my life straightened out for me."

"Don't mention it."

I liked the condo as soon as we drove up to it on Sunday morning. It was earth-toned and nondescript on the outside, but the first things you saw going in were the gas fireplace and huge windows in the living-room. The kitchen was small but since our cooking consisted of sandwiches and pasta, it didn't matter. Upstairs had two good-sized bedrooms and the bathroom. We went out to IKEA (Swedish for 'out of stock') that afternoon and I bought a bed and some bedding for it, and that was all I had to buy; Jude already had living-room furniture and all the dishes we needed.

I'd like it here, I was sure. It was nice to be back in town and it was very nice to be out of Vic Park. I wouldn't miss the hookers and the junkies and all that inner-city local colour stuff. And now I started to feel excited about school. After I got back from the admissions office Monday morning I spent most of the rest of the day poring over the calendar, deciding on courses. I felt so much better than I had for months. Years, maybe. Instead of feeling all fucked up and lost, I felt like I knew what I was doing for a change. I had a direction.

It took me a little longer to find a job, but within a couple of weeks I had some part-time hours at the U of C Bookstore. It was perfect, a job right on campus. In a bookstore, too. I was sure I'd like that. Everything was within walking distance of my rent-free home. Could things get any better?

Well, there was my love life, which was pretty sorry. But I just couldn't worry about it right then. I didn't have time to worry about it.

17. December 1984

Jude finished her exams the same day the bookstore closed down for Christmas holidays, Saturday, December 22nd. Her last exam was for a Stats course, and she'd crammed night and day for it. Sounded like it would be a killer. It ran from three to five in the Gold Gym and I worked until five.

Last day before Christmas was nuts at the bookstore, non-stop all day, and we were one person short. How the hell did I end up in retail again, I wondered, as I trudged home through the heavy, wet snow on aching feet. When I got home Jude wasn't there yet. She'd talked about maybe hitting Dinny's after the exam. So I decided to crash for a while.

I must have been a lot tireder than I thought, because I slept until almost nine o'clock. I had a sandwich and a bath, and then I felt a little more human. I slipped on the champagne-coloured silk satin pyjamas I'd bought a couple of weeks before. I'd always wanted some, and there was still all that Tuktoyaktuk money just begging to be spent. I really tried not to fritter it away, but I when I saw them in the lingerie shop window I just had to go in and touch them. And then I tried them on, and that was the end of it. If I could have, I would have worn them day and night.

Jude still wasn't back, but it wasn't even ten. She probably wouldn't be back for a long time yet. I settled down on the couch with a glass of wine and a collection of Donne's poetry and read for a while, but I couldn't keep my mind on it. I thought about the Christmas before, how we'd been up in Tuktoyaktuk. Things were very different, now. Life seemed comfortable, like things were falling into place, for the most part. Things weren't perfect, but I couldn't complain about much.

The snow fell more heavily around 10.45, when Jude came in.

"How'd the exam go?"

She sat down a little unsteadily on the bench beside the front door and took her boots off. "Oh, pretty good. It was actually a lot easier than I thought it would be. I finished by about 4.15."

She seemed tipsy, but not as bad as I expected. Not as bad as I probably would have been. "You haven't been in Dinny's since then, have you?"

"We stayed there for a while, but then we went to this girl Karin's place and had some pizza. It was okay. So how about you, how was work?"

"It was so fucking busy. It was insane. But it's over now, and I crashed for a while. I'm glad you made it, because I've been saving something the last few weeks until your exams were over." I reached into the pocket of my pyjamas and produced a fatty.

"Hey, all right. Well, I have a little something I've been saving myself. It's in the basement, but first I want to light a fire. Hang on."

After she lit the fire, fairly simple with a gas fireplace, she went downstairs and came back into the kitchen with a bottle of champagne, the real stuff. "Whoa, Jude. Dom Perignon, no kidding. Where'd you get this?"

She reached into the back of the cupboard and brought out two wine glasses. "I don't have champagne flutes, so I guess these will have to do. I bought it last week, 'cause I figured after exams finished we'd want to celebrate a little."

"Cool. I love champagne." I remembered the last time I'd had it, at a New Year's party with Niall, and put it out of my mind. Didn't want to think about that right then.

She poured some into each glass, and it foamed and bubbled like nothing else I'd ever seen. "C'mon," she said. "Let's take this into the living-room and spark up that joint."

"Good idea."

We smoked about half and put it out, stopped to see how it was working. I thought it was working, myself. I settled back into the couch and relaxed.

"How about a toast? To living together again?" Jude asked.

"Sure. Here's to living together again. It's been working out well." I had a sip of the champagne. "Holy shit. Is this stuff ever good. You must have spent a lot on it."

"Well, I thought for a special occasion it would be worth it. I'm celebrating."

"You must be happy exams are over."

"I am. But that's not really what I'm celebrating. I'm just pleased that you're here. I missed you so much last year."

"It's been good to be home. And to be here with you, Jude."

The champagne disappeared far too fast. I felt good; relaxed, happy, a little buzzed. Judith seemed strange—nervous, fidgety, spent a long time moving a pile of magazines from one table to another. I was about to ask her if everything was all right when she sat down again. She sipped at her drink, looked away from me. "I've been trying to think how to tell you this, Kate, and I just don't know how."

"Go ahead. I'm listening."

"Well, I find some old feelings are stirring up since you've been back. And it's hard to get them off my mind."

I twirled the glass around in my hand. "Feelings about me, you mean?"

"Yes. It can't have escaped your notice that...I don't know how to say this at all. I think I love you."

I didn't say anything for a minute. Not that I was shocked, but I wanted to be careful. I didn't want to say anything to hurt her. "Sometimes when we lived together before I wondered about that. But it didn't seem like it was an issue anymore, so I figured you'd forgotten about it."

"You were so wrapped up in Niall all that time."

"And you saw Mike for a long time. And other guys, too. In fact, I was always amazed. How did you do that?"

"Just lucky, I guess. But that doesn't mean I forgot about you. And now that you're back, I've been thinking about you a lot."

I felt strange now, uncomfortable, but not necessarily in a bad way. The pit of my stomach tightened. She watched me, tried to gauge my reaction. I considered for a moment what to say next. There had been clues, certainly. I had caught her looking at me a certain way, or for too long, sometimes. And I had to admit to myself that the idea had a certain appeal. Jude was an attractive woman, intelligent, fun to be with. But now, here it was out in front of us, like that, and I had to think what to say. I finally just ended up going with my gut. Not always the ideal course of action, but it is my usual modus operandi.

"I—well, I have to admit, I'm kind of curious. Really."

"Are you serious?"

"Sure. I mean, I can't tell you what I'll think about all this tomorrow. I don't even know that ten minutes from now I might not say stop, forget it. But right now, I feel a little adventurous. Why not? As long as you understand I can't make any promises." God, that sounded like something I'd heard somewhere before. From Niall, perhaps?

It was quiet for a minute, quiet enough that all we could hear was the fire crackling. In fact, it was so quiet I swear I could hear the individual snowflakes piling up on the roof.

She finally spoke. "You're not kidding, are you?"

"I wouldn't kid you about something like this."

She moved closer to me, slid her hand into mine and brushed the back of my hand against her cheek before kissing it. She put an arm around my shoulders, drew me close, lifted my chin for a kiss. A rather chaste kiss, I thought, but it was soon followed by hungry, demanding kisses. She pulled back. "I've wanted to do this for so long. I'm sorry, I can't seem to hold myself back."

95

I stroked her hair, tried to speak reassuringly. "It's all right. You don't have to hold back. Just relax. I'm not going anywhere. I'll be your baby tonight." Heh. Slipped some Bob in there and she didn't even notice.

I kissed her gently, stroked her cheek. Her hands slid over the satin on my back, then my thighs and belly. My nipples were hard when her hands reached them, and I shuddered as her warm, smooth hands explored.

"I love these pyjamas. They look fantastic on you."

"They feel nice on, too."

I slowly stood up as she opened the buttons down the front, pulled the drawstring at the waist open. The bottoms slid silently to the floor and Judith glided the top off my shoulders. I stood naked in the firelight, stroked her hair and shoulders. She ran her fingers along my hipbones and kissed my belly.

"My God," she whispered. "You're so beautiful."

"Thanks. You have a great body yourself," I answered, unzipping her jeans, fingering the buttons of her green sweater.

"I'm glad you think so." She kissed my nipples, kneaded my flesh like an old pro. Soon my knees were weak and I felt slick with excitement.

"So, Jude. Do you want to take me right here on the rug, or shall we go to bed?"

"Come to my bed."

I opened my eyes, looked around. What happened to my posters, my plants? I was a little startled when I realized where I was the next morning, and a little more startled when I turned over to see Jude smiling. It took me a second to remember how I got there in the first place.

"Good morning," I said, unsure whether a kiss was in order.

"Good morning," she said, as she leaned over and settled the matter. "How are you?"

I stretched, yawned, pulled the duvet up to my chin. "I feel good. And yourself?"

"Wonderful. I want to thank you for last night."

96

"You're welcome," I answered, and lit a cigarette. "So, uh, was I all right? I'm not sure what I'm supposed to do."

She slid her long, slim arms around me. "You were perfect."

18. June 1985

Jude and I went to a party at Chas Martin's place. Good old Chas Martin who used to be in Buick 57 lived in Crowchild Manor at the time, a huge turn-of-the-century brick house on Crowchild Trail, not far from the university. It must have been an impressive home at one time, but now it was a rooming-house, divided into creepy, dark little bachelor suites with shared kitchens and bathrooms. It was a party house, always crowded with the usual assortment of ACA students, drug addicts, musicians. Our friends.

Some of Jude's pals from her literary theory class, Laura, Lynn and Karin, came along with us. They drove me crazy. Laura was a round little bookworm, Karin was a tall, blond überjock. Lynn was all right, she was a little cooler than the other two. I probably shouldn't have let her cut my hair at 1.30 AM after we'd all been drinking, though. She cut it way too short. So short I thought about getting some electrical tape for my nipples and becoming a Wendy O. Williams impersonator. I hated the way it looked, but it was easy to take care of. Jude adored it. Anyway, what really drove me crazy about Jude's friends was this thing they had about the whole punk rock business. I always got the feeling they'd never listen to that kind of music at home, but they came to these parties and met these people in bands or formerly in bands, and wanted to hear all about the scene and "the old days." I mean, it was only a few years before. They kept bugging Jude to take them to The National, like they needed a guide or a sherpa or something to go and have a fucking beer at a bar.

Anyway, Chas' party was kind of weird, at least for me. For one thing, Maggie and Derek were there. I hadn't seen them in ages. I hadn't seen anybody in ages, what with school and full-time work. Maggie had a new job, bookkeeper at a construction firm, and seemed quite happy about it. And Derek was busy, busy, as usual. He was a journeyman by then, and he and a buddy started up their own welding company. Like grown-ups, these people. But they seemed to have grown-up problems, too. Something was definitely wrong. They were no longer the Maggie and Derek of yore, draped over each other and perpetually ready to sneak off somewhere. Maggie drank far too much that night and Derek sulked in a corner, didn't talk much at all.

"Everything okay between you guys?" I asked her.

"Things are fine. We're both a little tired. We've been working too hard."

"Maybe you need to go on a vacation."

"I think we do. But Derek doesn't want to go away in the summer. He says that's when all the building's going on."

"I guess that's true."

"What about you? How's it going?"

"Oh, being back at school is good. Last semester just flew. And now I'm working at the Bookstore for the summer, so that's cool."

"And how are things with Jude?"

I shrugged. How was it going? I didn't really know what to make of the whole thing, didn't know how I felt about it at all. I hadn't told many people about it. "Fine, I guess. I'm not sure."

"You're not happy?"

"I don't know what I feel about it, really."

"That doesn't sound good."

I almost said, *Maggie, why are we lying to each other? Why don't we tell each other what's really going on?* Instead, I just shook my head and said, "Yeah, I don't know."

We stayed out quite late. Not as late as Jude would have liked, but I wanted to leave at about 3.00. Late enough, no? But Jude was having a good time. I had an okay time too, until John Petersen from The Sisters showed up. I hadn't seen him since we'd dated briefly before Tuktoyaktuk.

I wore this black strapless, low-backed dress Jude loved. It was a nice dress. But she'd run her nails down my back while we stood and chatted to people. I hated it when she did things like that in public. I guess because I had mixed feelings about us. Sometimes I felt like the whole relationship was like Niall and me all over again, except in reverse. Like I was the one who was only in it for the sex. I didn't like feeling that way. Anyway, as she ran her nails down my back yet again, I heard a familiar voice. I turned around and there was John, giving me this look.

I left Jude and went over and talked to him. I hadn't seen him in ages, so we had a little catching up to do. He was working, had an apartment he said. And he looked good, he looked really good. He wore his hair a little longer than he used to, and he looked like he'd been working out, judging by the way his T-shirt fit. All the time we chatted, Laura, Lynn and Karin—the three weird sisters, I thought—eyed us suspiciously. I don't know what John thought, but I could just imagine. He didn't end up staying long, said he didn't think it was his kind of party. Then I wanted to leave, too.

It hit me then that even though I wanted to think I was totally open-minded, totally comfortable with this relationship, I wasn't. That was probably why I hadn't told many people about it. Carmen would freak out if she knew, and sometimes I felt like I was freaking out a bit myself. More and more I wondered why I was doing this. *The whole thing is crazy, isn't it?* And after a while the answer started to become clear.

19. July 1985

On the Saturday of the Canada Day weekend Jude convinced me we should go down to The National for old times' sake. I went along but didn't think I'd enjoy it. The place was too fraught, too numinous, had too many memories for me. And lately I felt I'd made some progress forgetting some of that stuff. She neglected to mention that Laura, Lynn and Karin would be there (I had to be careful not to call them 'the three weird sisters' out loud). I would have made up some excuse, any excuse not to come if I'd known they were coming. Of course that's why she didn't tell me. Sin of omission.

As it turned out I'd been right. I wasn't enjoying it, I told myself as I fixed my make-up in the mirror in the bathroom. Still, even though I was having a shitty time, I looked not too bad. Except for the hair.

"Wear the dress," Jude had suggested.

"The dress?"

"The one you wore to Chas' party. The black one. Could you?"

"I guess so." I wasn't sure I liked that. I didn't like the whole tone of things between us lately.

The National was crowded that night, the service was even slower than usual. The bands sucked. We sat right up front of the stage with Jude's pals, while Jude explained it all to them like they were tourists or something, like they'd never been out to see a band before. Which they probably hadn't, the grannies. And everything about the place, from the glasses of draft to the photocopied gig posters that still hung on one wall under a big sheet of heavy, clear plastic, made me think of the so-called old days. I even spotted an ancient XXX poster with a photo of the group. Niall must have been about seventeen in it. I wanted to try to steal it later, if I could figure out how to get it out from under that frickin' plastic. The whole thing depressed me.

On my way out of the washroom someone grabbed my arm from behind. I figured it was one of the old rummies from the pool table side of the bar. I yanked my arm away and turned to tell the offender off.

I caught my breath. "Niall—". He looked the same as always, wore his old leather jacket and jeans. A touch of stubble on his chin. His full lips curved in the same gentle smile. And immediately, I felt that old ache.

"I thought it was you," he said. "I wasn't sure for a minute. You look so different."

I self-consciously put a hand up to my shorn head. "What are you doing here?"

"Visiting my parents. I leave tomorrow. I'm just on my way out of here. Is this new?" he asked. He gently touched my left temple and ran his fingers through my bristly hair.

Please don't do that. I nodded.

"It's not you," he admonished.

"Damn you, Niall." Fuck. I'd been talking to him for 32 seconds and he had me on the brink of tears already. "I haven't seen you in two years and that's all you can say? That you don't like my hair?"

"Whoa, whoa. I'm sorry. I just meant I wouldn't have expected it. Listen, it's noisy in here. Let's go outside and talk a while."

I followed him out. How did he always manage to make me insane like that? We leaned up against a car in the parking-lot, side by side, our hips almost touched. I felt much better out there in the cool under the streetlights and the purple summer evening sky.

"So, how's school?" I asked.

"So far, so good. I'm halfway done my communications degree, and then I guess it's the faculty of law."

"You guess?"

"My dad is still set on it. I'm not so sure."

"What do you want to do?"

"Maybe travel a while. What about you? You're in school, right?

"Yeah, I'm in English at U of C. I saved up some money in Tuktoyaktuk and I'm living rent-free right now, so we'll see how it goes. School's expensive."

"You know it. And how was Tuktoyaktuk? You were there for a year, right?"

"Almost. I didn't have a great time. We got pretty good but we couldn't stand each other by the end. Had a disastrous affair with another musician. I'm a sucker for guys in bands, what can I say? So that was that. I went back to school almost as soon as we got back. So what else is new with you? Seeing anyone?"

"I was last year. It didn't work out. What about you? John

told me you're living with Judith. Sounds like a nice place."

I looked at him a long while. Just what had John said, I wanted to know? I turned away, looked across the street. "That sounded like more than one question. I am living with Jude, yes. And it is a nice place. I'm lucky. I could never afford school and rent."

"Kate?"

I looked back up at him. I felt miserable, but I couldn't even cry. *My life is a mess. I wanted so badly to see you again someday and tell you how great things are, tell you that I've finally found what I wanted. But my life is a huge mess, I realize now. I could never even tell you.*

"Are you all right?"

"Yeah, sure. I'm great."

He hugged me, brotherly-like. "I gotta go soon, so we'd better head back. It's been great seeing you, though. And you look really good. I didn't mean anything about your hair."

"Fuck off. It looks awful and you know it."

"I was just surprised. You never used to be so touchy."

We stopped just outside the back door of the bar. "There's my ride. Just a minute, Pete," he yelled to a man getting into a station wagon. "John said some strange things about you."

"John's a bastard. He's just mad because things didn't work out between us. But he's very trustworthy, you know. Whatever he said was probably true."

"I don't think it could have been. He must have just been mad."

"Maybe it was true. I don't know why you care. You left me, what does it matter to you what happens to me?"

"You know I care."

"You always tell me you care. And then you fuck off and break my heart."

He put his arms around me. *Please don't do this. I can't stand it.* "Goodbye, Kate. Take care of yourself." He kissed me, long and hard, a real Rhett Butler kind of kiss. What the fuck, I thought. What is this all about?

"Goodbye, Niall. Again."

I watched the car pull away, waved to him as it drove down the street and out of view. I walked back into the bar feeling numb.

"And how is the wonderful Mr. Graham?" asked Jude.

"He's fine."

"Lynn saw him accost you and drag you outside, so I felt I had to explain about him. I hope you don't mind," she said.

"Accost me? Oh, come on. Did you mention that I'd follow him anywhere if he'd let me?" My eyes stung.

"Well, that wasn't exactly what I said. C'mon, Kate, I didn't mean anything."

I picked up my purse, stood up. "I'll take a cab home. See you later."

That night I slept in my own bedroom, where I'd been the last few weeks, ever since the party at Crowchild Manor. When I got up around 9.30, there was no sign of Jude. I made some coffee and lounged around in my pyjamas. Smoked, read the paper. The sun flooded the condo that morning. For the first time in a long time, I felt like things were becoming clear to me. Soon she walked in, and looked like she hadn't slept much, and what sleep she got was with her clothes on. Well, it looked that way, anyhow.

"Good morning," she said, in a low voice.

"Good morning. There's some coffee on if you want some."

She poured herself a cup, sat at the table and cradled her head in her hands.

"Cigar? Cigarette?" I offered her my pack.

"Thanks. So, you look bright and chipper this morning."

I smiled self-righteously. "I got a good sleep last night. What about you?"

"We went over to Karin's after The National closed and drank some kind of cheap red wine in a box. Gala Keg or something."

"A gal a keg is enough for anyone. Isn't it?"

"Please. Have mercy. I think we finally went to sleep at about 4.30. Ouch."

"So, did the ladies like The National?"

"Oh, yes. They had a grand time. Very impressed."

"Well, that's nice. I always like to see people drink tables full of that old-time National draft. It just sets my heart aglow."

"Tables full, indeed. I know I've said it before, but I'll never drink that stuff again. Listen. I'm sorry about last night. I mean, what I said about Niall."

"Actually, I don't know what you did say about him."

"I just explained that he's your ex-lover. But I could have been nicer about it. I called him an asshole."

"Forget it. It doesn't matter. I feel great today. I forgot to check the mailbox Friday so I checked it last night when I got home, and you know what? I got a cheque."

"For what?" she asked foggily, as she searched for something in the cupboards.

"What are you looking for?"

"Tylenol."

"Above the sink."

She popped two tablets in her mouth, washed them down with a glass of water. "Thanks. So tell me about this cheque."

"I sold a piece of writing."

"You're kidding. That's great. I didn't know anything about this."

"I got a hundred dollars US for a 1500-word piece."

"No kidding? This is a magazine?"

"Yes. *Fantasy Magazine*."

"Fantasy? Like with dragons and wizards and that kind of thing?"

"No. More like whips and chains and that kind of thing."

Jude cocked an eyebrow. I never could do that, don't have that fine motor control in my forehead. I'd never be able to whip off a really effective *Fiddle-dee-dee*. "You'll have to let me read it. Congratulations."

"Thanks. I'm excited. There's something else, too, Jude. I've been thinking lately, about a change."

She sunk her face back into her hands for a moment, then looked up at me again with tired, glassy, hungover eyes. "I knew this would happen. It's been coming for a long time. What did it, finally? What did Niall say?"

"Niall said nothing. No, that's a lie, actually. He said he'd heard something strange about me from John. I don't know exactly what, but it must have been something about Chas' party. Remember? You had your hands all over me."

She coloured, spoke quietly. "I didn't have my hands all over you."

"You ran your nails up and down my back. Anyway, it doesn't matter. The point is, I started to think: if Niall had done that, I wouldn't have cared, probably would have enjoyed it."

"But you hate it when I do things like that, don't you?"

"I do. I feel like this isn't me. I guess I'm not curious anymore. I love you, Jude, I do. But not that way. It just isn't there." Why was it that every time I broke up with someone, I heard words Niall once said coming out of my mouth automatically, apparently of their own volition? And I'd say the same stupid thing every time, those same stupid words that seemed to have a life of their own. Goddammit.

"So it was just lust, is that it?"

"No, it wasn't just lust. I mean, that was part of it. Being needed was great, too. I don't know if I've ever really felt needed before. But it's just not enough."

"What will you do?" she asked.

"Live on my own for a while. You know, I've never lived by myself before. I think it'll be fun. Jude, don't cry."

She choked on her words. "I knew it was just a matter of time. I could see you weren't happy."

Neither of us spoke for a long while. I had to break the impasse.

"I'm sorry. I didn't want it to be like this. I'm so sorry."

Jude amazed me. I would have wailed, gnashed my teeth, thought of throwing myself in front of a train. She was upset, but could form sentences, didn't have great ropes of snot pouring from a red nose. How the hell did she do that, I wondered? "Don't be. I'm the one who should be sorry. I never should have pressured you into a relationship."

"You didn't pressure me. I entered it of my own free will. And I had some great times, didn't you?"

She nodded. "But I knew it wouldn't last. You are what you are, just like I am what I am, and you have to accept that. Don't you?"

"That's just it. And I know this isn't right for either of us."

"I know, I know," she sighed. "But it was so easy to forget about all those picky details and just concentrate on the good parts."

I smiled. "Now you sound like me."

Within a couple of weeks, I found myself a little apartment in Capitol Hill, not too far from the university or from Jude. We both tried to keep it sane and civil. Jude claimed she agreed that it was all for the best, that things weren't working out. Yet the coldness, the formality in our dealings made it clear how much she hurt. I agonized over how to deal with this.

The Sunday afternoon finally came when I had all my belongings out of the condo. This had little impact on the looks of the place. I'd have to scrounge up some furniture at the Salvation Army. Jude gave me a ride with the last of my stuff up to my new place, a second floor walk-up in a tiny nineteen-fifties apartment block. The one small bedroom contained my bed and my old thrift store lace sheers. Other than that, I had some floor cushions, a chair and a ghetto blaster in the living-room/kitchen area. And my typewriter.

"I feel terrible turning you out with no furniture like this."

"You're not turning me out. And I just haven't gotten around to getting stuff yet. Anyway, I have a bed, a chair, music, my typewriter. What else do I need?"

"Nothing, I guess. Nothing. It's a cute little place."

"It is. Jude, I've been trying to think what to say these last couple of weeks. I don't want to hand you the famous line about still being friends. But I do still want to be your friend. Sometimes, I wish this had all never happened, just because I'd hate for it to ruin our friendship."

She looked out the window. "I know. I've thought the same thing. We'll always be friends. Only right now, I still feel hurt. I'm getting better. I'm not there yet. But it's helped me make up my mind about something. I'll definitely go to library school next year."

"Hey, that's great. Where?"

"UBC, I think. I've applied there, anyway. The way I felt last week, I thought about doing my fourth year there. But I guess I'll wait and finish my bachelor's here. It would probably be simpler."

"My God, Jude. I didn't know you felt that bad."

"Don't worry. I'd thought about going, anyway. Now I know it's time for a new start for me, too." She sighed. "I'd better go."

"Thanks for driving me back and forth with this move." I gave her a hug. When I pulled back, her eyes looked wet.

"I have to go. Goodbye, Kate."

"Goodbye, Jude. Take care of yourself."

"You, too." She slipped silently out the door.

I watched her get into her car, waved. That didn't work out the way I envisioned it at all. Why was it that every time I broke up with someone, all I could think of to say were stupid clichés or things Niall said to me? No matter how carefully I thought about what to say before I said it, it always ended up sounding like a load of shit.

Fuck.

Entry #12   Saturday 10 Aug. 1985

So, I've been on my own for almost a week now. I like it, but I'm kind of lonely, too. I miss Jude in many ways, but in many other ways, I'm glad it's over. I feel a whole lot better, overall, but sometimes the guilt is overwhelming, partly because sometimes I think I was just in it for the physical gratification. What an evil hag I can be.

I've had lots more time to write since I've been alone. And I sold another piece, to BDSM Week out of San Francisco. I just have to be careful not to write myself into an erotica ghetto, never to emerge from the leather and chains. I mean, I don't intend to write this stuff all my life. But for now it's great, and it's fun. I seem to have had a surge of creativity the last week or so. There you go. Sometimes a change is as good as a rest, I guess.

Maggie came by one evening to see the new place. I hadn't seen her in a while, not since Chas' party. Dark hollows showed under her eyes, she looked thinner. Why is it that under stress the thin get thinner and the not-thin get not-thinner?

"Funny how we're both making new starts right now. I'm

leaving Derek," she said.

This didn't surprise me. "I got the idea things weren't working the last time I saw you guys."

She sighed. "It's been a long time coming. He's so possessive, so controlling. Wants to tell me what I should do, who I should do it with. And he only gets worse as time goes by. I've had it. I've been getting rid of my stuff, and I've got it down to what I can fit in a backpack. Tomorrow, I'm leaving."

I didn't like the sounds of this. "Where are you going?"

"I'm hitting the road. Heading to Vancouver."

"Have you got a ride to the airport?"

"I'm hitchhiking."

"You're not really. It's dangerous for women to hitchhike."

"You sound like Derek. Don't you guys think I know how to take care of myself?"

"It's not that. You just never know who you'll get a ride from."

"You think I'll get in a car with Clifford Olson or something?"

"You can't tell from looking at people what they're like. Look, if you need some money for a ticket—"

"It's not the money. I have money. I just want to get out there and be free for a while. I'm tired of living my life according to other people's expectations. You should have a job, you should make this much money, you should be married, you should have kids. And anyway, I think I happen to be a good judge of character. I have a certain intuition about them. I'll be able to tell if people are bad news, don't worry."

"I don't know. I know someone you could talk to, maybe help you sort things out before you go."

"Not you too, Kate!"

"Maggie. You have to face reality."

"So do you! Who do you think you are, telling me what to do, telling me how I should act?"

"Who do I think I am? I'm someone who loves you."

"If you loved me, you'd fuck off and leave me alone."

I sighed. "Look, I'm sorry. I don't want you to go away mad at me. Never mind what I said. I'll miss you, you know."

"I'm sorry, too. And you know I'll miss you. But we'll keep

in touch, don't worry."

Something made me wonder, after she left that night, if I'd ever see her again. I wondered, too, if I'd ever see the Maggie I used to know again. This Maggie was so defensive and hostile, and she seemed to be just running blind. I hoped she knew what she was doing. And I hoped she'd be all right.

20. April 1986

I thought I would hate Gabriel Ruiz's Seventeenth-Century Poetry class when I enrolled in it in third year, but it turned out to be one of my favourites. He had a sense of humour and seemed to have a real personal interest in the course material. He was younger than most of the other profs, much better looking and also appeared to have many items of clothing in his wardrobe. This alone put him ahead of his colleagues. He wore his thick, wavy black hair combed straight back from his forehead, his eyes were velvet black and a small gold hoop in his left ear accented his warm gold complexion. I found him charming, as did many of my fellow students, but I never seriously thought about acting on my attraction to him. At the end of term I got my final essay in the course back with a note requesting an interview in his office. Shit, I thought, now what? I made an appointment with his secretary and saw him the next day.

"Hello, Dr. Ruiz. I'm Kate Brandt, from your 312 class. You wanted to talk to me about my essay?" I felt awkward as I stood in the doorway of his tiny, windowless office, too big for it, like Alice after eating that cake. Stacks of books and papers covered every available surface, and the only thing on the wall was a large portrait of the poet Pablo Neruda. At the time, I had no idea who it was.

"Come in," he said, and shook my hand while he removed a pile of papers from a chair. "You like my portrait of Neruda?" he asked, noticing me noticing it.

"It's very nice."

"Do you like his work?"

"Oh, yeah. He's great. Very seminal." I didn't want to sound like an idiot.

"Sit down," he encouraged me, and closed the door. "It wasn't really your essay I wanted to talk about. I wanted to discuss your academic future." The air felt hot, close, stale. My knees almost touched his, though the back of my chair touched the wall opposite him.

"Well, at the moment, I'm afraid I don't have much of an academic future."

"That's exactly what I want to talk about. I heard from Dr. Crane that you're not returning next year."

Why had they been talking about me? "That's right. I want to come back sometime. But right now, I can't afford it. Even with student loans and part-time work, I'm always short. It'll just have to wait a few years, until I can save some money. If I can get something else in addition to the part-time work I'm doing now, I should be able to do it." The Tuktoyaktuk money was now just a fond memory. But, oh, baby, the times we had together.

"Do you mind if I ask what you're doing part-time?"

"Working at the Bookstore. And doing some writing."

"What kind of writing?"

"Freelance stuff for magazines."

"And you get a steady income doing it?"

"Well, not that steady. That's the problem. It adds up to a few hundred a month, usually."

His face lit with genuine interest. I was also interested, in the straight, white teeth I noticed when he smiled. "That's fantastic. What magazines do you write for?"

"I don't know that you would have heard of any of them."

"I'm pretty well-read. Try me."

"I write erotica," I told him. The room seemed to get smaller and smaller, suddenly. Where was that Drink Me bottle, anyway?

He waited for an explanation, a punchline, perhaps. After a moment he asked, "You're not joking, are you?"

"No, I'm not. I've been doing it, writing it I mean, for a

while now. Well, for money, I mean."

"Interesting. You seem ashamed, though."

Why didn't I just tell him I worked at Burger King? My mouth was sandpaper. "Not ashamed. Maybe embarrassed."

"Please, Ms. Brandt—may I call you Kate?"

"Sure."

"And please call me Gabriel. Kate, you should be proud. Do you think there might be a chance you could keep up your studies if I could help you find a part-time position in the English department? I happen to know of one coming up. Just a clerical thing, but it might interest you." He felt no shyness about running his gaze up and down the length of my legs.

I cleared my throat. "I'd have to find out about the pay and the hours and so on before I could answer, but it sounds good."

"I'd be happy to look into it for you. You can call me back here around four tomorrow—you do have my office phone number, don't you?—and I'll let you know what I found out. I'd hate to see you leave just because of a little thing like money."

"Money isn't such a little thing when you don't have any. But thanks for your help. Do you always take such a personal interest in your students' affairs?"

"Not always."

I wished I hadn't asked him that. I waited for some explanation, other than his eyes undressing me. I knew it wasn't my exceptional marks.

He cleared his throat. "Listen, what are you doing this evening?"

I stared at him for a few seconds. He continued. "I'm sorry. I don't mean to offend you."

"Not at all. You just caught me by surprise. Tonight I'm…not doing much of anything."

"I wonder if you'd want to join me for a drink?"

We met, not at the Faculty Club as I first suspected we might, but at a bar not far from campus. Of course when I thought about it later I realized we couldn't go to the Faculty Club.

How would that have looked?

"So, I suppose you bring all your student friends up here," I said after our drinks arrived.

"I don't have so many friends among the students."

"Maybe not, but you have a lot of admirers."

He rolled his eyes. "Yes, the young ladies do seem to sit up and take notice of me. When we get to those sonnets they all swoon in their seats. I suppose you were one of them."

"Be fair. I never swooned. But I did notice you right away. You do sort of, ah—stand out from your colleagues."

He smiled, fidgeted with the napkin under his beer glass. "I noticed you right away, too, you know. You remind me of a renaissance angel."

"A what?"

"A renaissance angel. Like you might see in a painting by Leonardo or Titian. Except you're here, in one of my classes."

"You are quite a flatterer, Gabriel."

"I mean it. So I've wanted to meet you, find out more about you, ever since term began. And what I find so far is interesting. An angel who writes erotica."

"Yes, well, I don't talk about it much. But it pays the rent. Almost."

Later, he dropped me off at my apartment. "Have you ever read San Juan de la Cruz?" he asked.

"No. Should I have?"

"Well, talk about erotic writing. I'm sure you'd find it interesting. Would you like to come up to my place Friday night and I could read some of it to you?"

"That does sound interesting."

Entry #15   Sun. 3 May 1987

Last night, Gabriel took me out for dinner. We went to an Italian place in Bridgeland, had some wonderful food and wine. Then we went to his place.

He has a condo near the university, not far from where Jude and I lived, funnily enough. When we arrived he poured us a couple more glasses of wine, put on some music, and kissed me, once. Then he stepped back and said, "I'm going to take a shower. Could you wait a few minutes for me?" As if I'd leave.

While he showered, I looked around, enjoyed the music. He'd put on Stan Getz, saxophone tickling my ear like a lover's hot breath, making the hairs on the back of my neck stand straight up. I felt nervous like a virgin, trembled until he came out in his bathrobe and stood behind me, slipped his hands down my back, bit the nape of my neck. I still get shivers thinking about it.

What a fantastic night. He is hot, let me tell you.

He did read me some San Juan de la Cruz, and I borrowed the book from him. He's right, it is erotic.

"En mi pecho florido, que entero para él solo se guardaba, allí quedó dormido, y yo le regalaba, y el ventalle de cedros aire daba," he read, from a poem called "Noche Oscura." It sounded hot even before I knew what it meant. Of course, he could read the phonebook in Spanish and it would sound hot. He translated it for me: "On my flowering breasts which I had saved for him alone, he slept and I caressed and fondled him with love, and cedars fanned the air above." Whoa. Who would have ever thought a sixteenth-century Castilian monk could come up with stuff like that? Before, it seemed I'd been disappointed too many times in the past to let myself go overboard with excitement, anticipation. Gabe's brought that all back again. Being in love again is amazing. Holy shit, it's great.

21. May 1990

We couldn't decide where to have the wedding. It wasn't between a church and City Hall. A church wedding was right out. I wasn't one of these heathens who can suddenly after years of amoral bliss turn around and get married in a church like nothing happened all those years and I didn't even need to go to confession. I was a devout heathen. Gabe, too, San Juan de la Cruz notwithstanding.

What we couldn't decide on was the country—Canada or El Salvador. Finally, we decided that if we went to El Salvador his family, specifically his mother and older sister Maria, would make a huge deal out of it. And we didn't want it to be a huge deal. Of course, Carmen could be counted on not to make a huge deal of it.

While my mother and I had reconciled to some degree over the years, our relationship really improved when I told her we were marrying. Gabriel performed this miracle. He talked me into dropping in on my parents one day, on the pretence of announcing our engagement. He charmed her, melted her icy old booze-addled heart. They flirted with each other, even. How cute. And my parents seemed much better by this time. From what I could tell they drank a lot less, so naturally everything else in their lives improved, or so it appeared. They didn't fight as much anymore, I don't think, and Carmen seemed generally more reasonable. She was less sarcastic and critical when I talked to her, wasn't as moody. She was like a different person.

So much had changed in the last few years, sometimes I wondered whose life this was. I continued working in the U of C English department until I finished my degree, then I got a full-time job in the admissions office. Maybe not a dream career, but it paid off the student loan and allowed me time at night and on the weekends to write. So life had finally settled into something stable. I felt like I had a base, a foundation, the secure home I'd been looking for, for the first time in my life.

We decided to have the wedding in Calgary and go to El Salvador for our honeymoon. We had the ceremony at the house we rented in Sunalta, in the southwest, near downtown. The day was warm and still, the sky was clear and blue so we had the ceremony under the huge poplar tree in our backyard. It stayed warm until sunset, and then we moved the party inside. Gabe's sister Maria came all the way to Calgary, with her husband Carlos and three year-old son Ernesto; I met the rest of the family on the honeymoon. Jude made it in for the occasion, and so did Maggie. She arrived several hours late, as was her wont, and alone. I wanted to talk to her, but I didn't get a chance to say much. I didn't get a chance to talk to anybody for all that long. Too much was going on with gifts and guests and caterers and relatives, having to greet and pose and goodbye and open stuff and have the odd glass of champagne and all that. By the time Gabe and I were left alone to celebrate our wedding night, I was dead tired. Well, okay, not *that* dead tired.

Maggie hadn't been back to Calgary since she hit the road back in '85. A few months after she left, she called me.

"Hey, Maggie! It's good to hear from you again. How's Vancouver?"

"Oh, it was great. But I'm in San Francisco, now. You'd love it down here. So many things to do all the time, so many interesting people. Came down here with some friends I met in Vancouver."

We ended up talking for over an hour about hitchhiking out to Vancouver, about her new friends, about San Francisco. It sounded like she was enjoying herself, but it didn't exactly sound like she was working or anything. I wondered how she was paying for the phone call.

"There you go again, Kate. You've turned into a real worrier. I have a friend who's covering my expenses right now."

"That's handy. I should get a friend like that."

She laughed as if I'd just told a great joke. I didn't have the heart to tell her I didn't get it.

A couple of years later Maggie moved to Seattle. I don't know what it was, but she seemed annoyed with me, almost angry, every time I called her. I thought maybe if I went to visit her in person things would be better. When I arrived at her place I thought I might have had the wrong address at first, because the apartment building the cab driver took me to looked expensive, stylish. I got him to wait outside just in case. But no, it was Maggie's place, all right.

I looked around at the leather sofas, the hardwood, the minimal decoration, the track lighting. And the place was spotless. I didn't understand. Did she actually live there? Not alone. If this was really Maggie's place, it would be the usual disaster area. But I started to ask questions, discreetly so as not to set her off, and it seemed to be true. She lived there by herself. She was doing some "consulting," remained mysterious about what kind of work it was. Finally I had to ask her secret.

"Okay. You've got to have a housekeeper, right? It's so clean."

"I wondered when you'd notice."

"I noticed right away. I've just been trying to figure it out. It looks great."

"I have one of my men do it for me."

"Men?"

She laughed. "I have one look after my car, one decorate, one clean. Of course, a girl like yourself has an entire lifetime of housework to look forward to. You're smart to just accept that and learn how to do it well. But I can influence others without even speaking to them, as you know." Actually, this was news to me, but she continued before I could say anything. "I just kept sending messages to Darren, and then one day he started to clean, unbidden." She leaned over and added confidentially, "That's the kind of power I have over men." Something had definitely happened to Maggie since she moved. Was it the water on the West Coast? Or had her days with Derek been a brief interlude of seeming calm, a fluke, perhaps?

I nodded, imagined poor Darren, whoever he was, one of Maggie's current beaux apparently, realizing he'd have to clean the bathroom himself if he wanted it clean. Many times I'd thought of cleaning Maggie's bathroom before using it, too. But then perhaps I'd also been the unwitting recipient of her messages.

I took a shot at finding out how she could afford the place. "I love your apartment. You must be doing pretty well at your job. What did you say you were doing again?"

"Consulting. I work from home. Business is good right now."

"What kind of consulting, Maggie? Tell me what you're doing. Really."

She looked me in the eye. "What do you think I do?"

I fumbled for the right words. "I think you're a call girl." 'Call girl' sounded stupid, but I just couldn't bring myself to say prostitute.

She didn't say anything for a second. "That's one way of

putting it. A call girl, an escort. And I'm a very successful one. I've been doing it for a couple of years now."

An image of Katya's dead body flickered in my mind. Could Maggie end up like that, too? "Do you ever think about getting some help?" I asked. I knew this would probably make her mad, but I felt like I had to throw it out there.

"I am NOT crazy," she told me. "In fact, I think if anybody's crazy here, it's you." Her nostrils flared, her eyes were wild. I did a quick check for sharp objects and wished I could rewind the tape. And me without life insurance.

"Maggie, I didn't say anything about crazy. I said you might need some help."

"You're projecting. You're the one that needs help. You're just jealous of me, you always have been. And you come around here and judge my lifestyle. "

"I probably do need help. But I'm not judging you. I'm concerned. I can't help thinking about Katya."

"Katya? What I'm doing and what Katya did are two completely different things. You can't compare me to her!"

"I'm sorry, Maggie. I'm just trying to understand. Why didn't you tell me before?"

"Because I knew you wouldn't understand. I knew you'd react like this, calling me crazy, telling me you don't approve of me. You won't accept me the way I am."

"No, it's not you that I don't approve of. It's just—"

"What I do, right?"

I sighed. "I don't think you need to do it, that's all."

"What if I want to do it? I should stop just because you think it's immoral?"

"I didn't say it was immoral. I think it's bad for you."

"You've done plenty of things that are immoral and bad for you, and I didn't judge you!"

She was so defensive. Everything I said or tried to say she twisted and turned back on to me. I got frustrated, angry with her. "I think it's pathetic," I said, "that you can't see what you're doing to yourself. When are you going to wake up?"

"Who's pathetic?" she asked, turning things back on me again.

"You know, Maggie, I think there's no point to this conversation anymore. I'm leaving."

"That suits me."

Outside her building I caught a cab to go to the airport. Things shouldn't have gone like that, and it was my fault. I should have been nicer. But it was the shock of finding out what she was doing. I didn't know what to say, how to proceed. Were we no longer friends? If so, did that now mean we were enemies? It felt like it.

In the months after our wedding, I started to piece together a strange collage of my old friend, bizarre pieces from different sources. Most of our guests had never met Maggie before, and I kept hearing things like "Who *was* that woman?" and "What was she on?" I heard about the strange things she told our guests, the single male ones that is, about being able to communicate with beings from other worlds and the spiritual value of possessing a large thong collection. Had she been that drunk?

The strangest piece of the collage came a few months after the wedding. One day I got a postcard from Maggie, on holiday in L.A. with some boy toy, and Gabe saw it as he went through the stack of mail.

"Maggie's a strange woman," he told me.

"Oh, yeah."

"I got a copy of our video from Peter today. Come and have a look at it."

One of Gabe's pals had shot some video of our wedding party. The footage of Maggie was telling. She sat alone on the couch in the crowded living-room. A buffer zone of about five feet surrounded her in all directions; she'd been at the party long enough for the other guests to learn to stay away from her. My heart ached for my old friend when I saw this, and yet I could understand it. I think if I'd just met Maggie at a party, I wouldn't talk to her for long, either. I saw, too, why people kept asking me what she was on. On the video she had some kind of strange fake smile plastered on her face. And her eyes. Her eyes looked so strange. They bugged out of her head, glassy, whites huge. I couldn't imagine what drug causes that. Maybe it wasn't a drug at all.

22. November 1994

I lay in bed late one Saturday morning while Gabe watched some kind of sports on TV. I hate sports on TV. I mean, who came up with the idea that it should be News, Sports and Weather, as if sports are so important in most people's lives? How about News, Art and Weather? News, Music and Weather?

In spite of his fondness for watching footage of steroid monsters chasing pieces of rubber, I loved Gabe. The three years we'd been married had been the happiest of my life. He was handsome, attentive, caring, intellectually stimulating, wonderful in bed. Even Carmen and Dad liked Gabe. Of course, nobody's perfect, not even Gabe. One of his major flaws was that he was a serious writer.

At a book launch we'd gone to a few months before, he introduced himself and me to the author, saying he was a writer who taught at the university and I worked in the admissions office. Was it my imagination, or had he been like this only since he'd got tenure the year before? Later, I mentioned it.

"I wonder sometimes why you couldn't introduce me as a writer? I mean, you said you were a writer, but not me."

"I'm sorry. I had no idea you'd take offence at that. I didn't mean any harm. I guess what I meant is that I'm a serious writer."

"And I'm not?"

"Not yet, my Kate. You're too young."

"So, I guess until I have a couple of volumes of poetry out, like you do, I'm just a hack."

"I didn't say that."

I was outraged with him over that for days. Even so, in many other respects, I felt lucky to have him. We still rented the house in Sunalta, and were looking at buying a house somewhere near the university.

All us ex-Misclairol gals were getting old, I guess. I saw

Clare now and then. She'd been married for a few years, to Bryan, a nice and not at all difficult to look at geologist. After getting a degree in Philosophy she taught guitar, and loved it. I'm sure she was good at it. She was always patient with me. Our drummer Wendy had married a DJ at CJAY 92, and I heard she was pregnant. I heard even Barb, our first bass player, had settled down to domestic bliss out in Toronto, planned to have a family. Debbie, our second bass player, had gone to law school and worked in family law. And here I was, gainfully employed, married and soon to be mortgaged. Could life get any more respectable and responsible?

Well, it could. I became obsessed with having a baby. I seemed to have a hell of time getting pregnant (I couldn't help thinking of that now-ironic scare with Niall). And when I did get pregnant, it didn't seem to take. I had three miscarriages in two years, always around nine weeks. The first time upset me. The second time I felt worse. I got more frustrated, it got harder to take every time. I knew it put a strain on our relationship. Now, sex had become so fraught with implication, so geared toward procreation (the romance of thermometers, mucous charts), that the fun slowly drained out of it. Sex became work. Who knew this could happen?

I'd been for a test a couple of weeks earlier and I was pregnant again, about eight weeks along. This wasn't like the other times, so far: I felt different. This time I had morning sickness, my breasts ached, I had some strange food aversions. The idea of avocados, which I normally loved, turned my stomach and I couldn't stand the smell of toast. I'd been let down by my body too many times now to take these as good signs and let myself get excited, but I allowed myself the luxury of a small, private hope at the same time.

A few days later, early in the afternoon while I was at work, it happened again. I felt the contractions come on in the morning, knew it would happen, tried to pretend it wouldn't. Even before I could leave the office, it was over. Another failure. All my hopes lost again in a rush of blood. Disappointment, frustration, anger numbed me. I couldn't even cry until I got into my car. I figured I'd see my doctor the next day. She'd probably want me to have another D & C. But I didn't want to think about that right then. I only wanted a shower and a sleep at that moment, couldn't think any further.

When I turned onto our street, I saw Gabe's car in front of the house. Why was he home at this time of day? I didn't have to wonder long. When I got in, the stereo was on. Stan Getz, I noted. A half-empty bottle of wine and two emptied glasses stood on the coffee table. The sound of giggling came through the open bedroom door. And Gabe, I knew, was no giggler.

I stood still for a moment, tried to decide what to do. Should I leave? And where would I go? Back to work? Home to mother? Get on a plane for somewhere? Hell, no. I stormed down the hallway to our bedroom.

"Hello, Gabriel."

I hadn't caught them in the act, exactly. This scene was obviously post-act. Gabe and a young redhead lay entangled, looked languid, exhausted. And probably happy before I arrived. Now the girl squirmed, her face reddened while my husband's grew pale.

"What are you doing home?" he wanted to know. As if I'd done something wrong.

"I live here, remember? I'm sick, so I'm home from work early." I couldn't tell him about the miscarriage, not now. I'd have fallen apart if I told him that, and I wouldn't, not in front of that girl. "I guess I don't need to ask why you're here." I turned to the girl, who dressed hurriedly. "Let me guess: English 312? Did he read San Juan de la Cruz to you?"

"That's enough, Kate," he said.

"You're telling me that's enough. I think it's time you got out of here!"

The girl ducked out the door. Gabriel dressed now. "You need to calm down," he said in a low voice.

"Fuck you! You need to get a conscience. Get out of my fucking house," I screamed, as I tore the sheets off the bed and threw them at him.

He left. I showered, and spent the next few hours on the couch, tried to rest, tried to feel better. I cried on and off, not as much as I would have expected. When I did cry it was mostly about the baby. I poured myself a glass of wine from the half-empty bottle on the coffee table and began to make a pile of Gabe's possessions in the middle of the living-room floor. Clothes, books, records, everything. I couldn't decide whether to leave them there for him to remove or to make a bonfire out of them. The bonfire idea appealed to me more, but probably wasn't very practical. One thing I knew was that he'd have to leave. I knew he'd try to argue, but he had to leave.

He came back about 10.30 that night. I'd slept awhile in the afternoon, and now I drank wine, flipped through magazines. Tried to think what to say to him.

He hung up his coat and sat on the arm of the couch, looked wordlessly at the pile of his belongings. "Is this a message?" he finally asked.

"It is. A subtle message, like the one you gave me today."

He gave me a sharp look. "You're drunk!"

"Yes, I am. But to paraphrase Winston Churchill, I'll be sober in the morning and you'll still be an asshole." I didn't want to start out being sarcastic but I couldn't help it, couldn't sound any other way except how I felt: hurt, outraged.

"No, I mean you shouldn't drink right now."

"Oh, don't worry about that. As of this morning, I am no longer pregnant. Again."

"I'm sorry. Why didn't you tell me?"

"I didn't want to get into it with your little friend around."

He sighed. "I don't think you understood at all what went on today."

"What's to understand?"

"What I mean is, I don't love that girl. I love you. You know I do. She means nothing to me."

"Funny way to show me you love me."

"It's just that things are so different between us now. The joy, the spontaneity are all gone."

"So you just thought you'd have some joyful, spontaneous sex elsewhere. Or with someone else, I should say. You're still doing it in the same place."

"All I mean is that I didn't know what I was doing. But please listen to me." He sat beside me now, took my hand, looked into my eyes. He'd only forgotten the box of chocolates and the bunch of flowers. Actually, I could have done with some chocolate right about then. "I can't tell you how sorry I am. What happened today will never happen again, I promise you." He smiled, waited for me to warm up. He seemed to think he could do a little time in El Casa del Fido and then everything would be all right again.

"You must think I'm an idiot. What makes you think I'll forgive and forget this? No way. This marriage is so over."

He got angry. "When we first met, I got the impression that you were sexually freer than you really are."

"What made you think that? My writing?"

"Yes. But now I can see you're completely provincial."

"Fuck you. I suppose you think sleeping around makes you sophisticated. And how strange to have to explain to you of all people that the writing is not the same as the writer."

"You're impossible to understand. You're a little girl who writes erotica and has the sexual mores of an old woman. And you think that *Gone With the Wind* is great literature."

"That's it, Gabriel. First, you sleep with a girl in our bed when I'm at work. While I'm having a miscarriage, no less. And then you insult me. Now you listen to me: get out of here. Take your shit and get out of here—no, no, don't even think about interrupting. This discussion is over, everything is over. Get your stuff out of here by the end of the week or I'll sell it. And after that, I don't ever want to see you again. My lawyer will be in touch with you."

His face darkened. The muscles in his cheek rippled, his nostrils flared and for just a second I felt a little afraid, unsure of what he might do. "You can't afford to live here by yourself," he finally said.

"That's a minor point. I'll either get a roommate or move. Do you think I would stay with you after what you did to me today, because I can't afford to live alone? Now please leave. I need to get some sleep."

"What, you mean leave tonight?"

123

"Yes, tonight. Now. Go sleep in a hotel, or in your girl-friend's dorm. You just can't sleep here."

Without another word, he put his coat on and slammed the door behind him.

At first I thought I'd be able to keep my job. But as the weeks went by I knew that sooner or later I'd run into Gabe. And there were too many reminders of him around the university. I decided to quit. I handed in my notice a week before the Christmas holidays. My supervisor was sympathetic, and arranged to have me laid off so I could collect unemployment insurance.

So 1995 started with new beginnings, though not the ones I'd wanted. I moved to a tiny apartment in Bridgeland, still close to downtown. I had no job. I planned to stay on UI as long as I could and try to use the time to write, and recover.

Strangely, I didn't feel the way I expected to. In the old days, if all this had happened, I would have felt devastated, like I'd die. Like I did when Niall left. Now I felt more shock, numbness. Certainly, I was sad and angry at times. But mostly I felt just numb. Compared to being broken-hearted, it wasn't such a bad way to feel.

23. Summer 1995

Although Carmen and I were getting along better, she was no help at all after my marriage fell apart. Big surprise. Oh, sometimes she'd be on my side, but most of the time she blamed me. I worked too much, didn't look after his needs well enough, put too much pressure on him about the whole baby thing. I don't think she had any idea how much I'd wanted to have a baby. Dad had left her a few months earlier and I knew that was probably part of the problem, that she was struggling with that. Still, it hurt to be on the skids with her again, to lose the little bit of progress we'd made with our relationship. We stopped calling each other. I almost called her many times but something stopped me. Pride or stubbornness. Or maybe it all hurt me more than I wanted to admit. I wondered sometimes if Niall hadn't felt that way about calling me.

Then I started to dream about her a lot. They weren't really recurring dreams, but for a couple of months certain features were constant: she lived somewhere close by, always to the west of my apartment, but purposely avoided me. She seemed to be slipping away from me, trying to hurt my feelings somehow. I woke up annoyed, hurt, confused.

One night I had a particularly vivid dream where she hung around and peered at me through the apartment windows. I would just see her in my peripheral vision but whenever I tried to look directly at her, she'd be gone. In the morning, I finally decided that enough was enough, and I had to call her. No answer. When I called back later there was still no answer, so I left a message.

For a couple of days I left messages. I knew her. She was probably just not answering to be difficult. I started to think she could even be drunk, although she'd been good lately. I finally decided to go check on her.

When I got there, she didn't answer the front door. I went around to the back, thought she might be in the yard. She wasn't, but the back door was unlocked and as I went in I saw the flicker of the TV.

So she was drunk, I thought. The tube blared. The good old bottle of rye and empty ice cube tray sat on the kitchen counter. I went into the living-room and switched off the TV. Carmen lay on the couch, empty glass and full ashtray at her side. Some things never change, I thought, annoyed, unsure whether I wanted to wake her up or not. She could be bitchy as hell when woken up under these circumstances. But since I came all the way over I decided I might as well rouse her.

Her hand was cold when I touched it. I pulled my hand away, stood back. She wore a sleeveless nightgown, and I noticed that the underside of her greyish arm, where it lay along the couch, was purple. For a moment I wondered what the hell could be wrong, what would do that, when the answer suddenly rushed in on me like a wave.

I called 911, as if seconds counted at this point. Even though the paramedics took only a few minutes to arrive, it seemed like a long time. I knew she was dead, but even when they told me she'd been dead for a while, maybe a couple of days, I couldn't believe it. After that things are a blur. I called Dad at work and he came over right away. I was grateful he came, so relieved to see him because I didn't feel capable of doing anything. We stood and held onto each other and cried a long time.

That night I tried to call Jude, but her new partner Alicia said she was on her way to the Canadian Library Association conference in Toronto. She called the next morning, though.

"Kate. Alicia told me what happened. I'm so sorry."

"I can't really believe it yet. I'm in total shock."

"I'm sure you'll feel like that for a while. Listen, I don't think I'll be able to make it out there for the funeral. I'm really sorry."

"Don't worry about it, Jude. Dad says she didn't want much of a funeral anyway. I guess we'll have it late next week. I'm not sure yet."

"I can take some time off in a couple of weeks, though. Can I come and see you then?"

"It'd be great to see you."

"Good. I'll let you know once I have a flight and everything."

And two weeks later Jude lugged her suitcase out of the cab, down the stairs and into the Unicorn, where I'd suggested we meet. She spotted me in the corner booth where we used to sit, already well through a pint. No longer the Renaissance angel of my wedding day, I looked like fucking hell. I hadn't washed my hair in a while, the dark (and grey) roots were almost two inches long. I couldn't be bothered with makeup, it cut into my smoking time too much. I wore the least smelly clothes I could find on my bedroom floor: a baggy black sweater and baggy jeans, to hide my baggy body. Jude, on the other hand, cut a trim, impressive figure in her beige linen suit, hair looking sleek, professional. People must have thought she was my parole officer or something. We embraced for the first time in a long while. Then I stood back at arm's length and took a good look at my friend.

"Jude, you look fantastic."

"Well, thanks. So do you."

We sat. "Ah, thanks anyway. How was your flight?"

"Fine. So how are you, Kate? Do you want to talk about what happened?"

I lit a cigarette. "I do." I took a long sip of my McEwen's for fortification. "It was an awful shock to find her there like that. I mean, all my life I've expected her to die in a car accident or pass out with a lit cigarette, or for her liver to just plain give out. A heart attack, I never expected."

"You seem to be dealing with it pretty well."

"I am and I'm not. I can talk to you about it. To lots of other people I couldn't. In one way, it amazes me that Carmen lived as long as she did. But she was only 49, so I feel cheated in a way. And yet deep down there's a part of me, a little horrible, evil part of me, that's kind of glad she's gone."

"I don't think that's so strange, considering your child-hood."

"Not even glad, really. Relieved is more like it. But then I feel guilty for even thinking things like that."

"You have nothing to feel guilty about."

"It's hit me a lot harder than I would have expected. You know, she was kind of absent in my life for such a long time. Of course, maybe that's why I'm really feeling it."

"Sure. You probably feel ripped off. How's your dad?"

"He's been living on his own the last six months. I mean, he still felt broken up about it, but he's not as bad as he would have been before the separation. And you know, that son-of-a-bitch Gabe didn't even show up at the funeral. He called and said he'd come, but then he didn't."

"He's a class act. And he has bad sperm to boot."

"Why do I always have to fall in love with a man before I find out what an asshole he is? Pretty poor screening system I have here."

"If you'd known, you wouldn't have married him, right?"

"No, I guess not. The worst part is, I thought I finally had

127

it together. I thought Gabe could give me happiness, security, provide me with that still centre to my life that I've been looking for. Ha. All this bullshit he tried to hand me about having papers to mark, not being able to be at home nights. He could have marked them at home, I said. Too many distractions at home, he'd say. Talk about distractions at home. I thought he meant *me*. Come to think of it, I guess that's what he did mean. And it was only seven months ago, the little bastard. Why does everything happen all at once?"

"I don't know. I find life has a funny way of doing that. You go along for years and nothing ever happens to you, and then all this shit happens, one trauma after another, and then things get sort of back to normal."

"And you spend the next five years recovering. Well, here's to that. I'll buy us another round."

The day before Jude left town, she came to my apartment.

"I'm glad you're here," she said after I opened the door.

I was a little drunk, just enough to take the edge off things. I'd worn the same grey sweatsuit for some time. Newspapers, pizza boxes and empty beer cans covered most available surfaces in the apartment. The drawn curtains blocked out the sun, and a video flickered on pause.

"Are you okay?" she asked, and cleared a space on the couch so she could sit. "I've been trying to call you all day."

"I've been here—oh, shit, that's right. I turned the phone off when I watched *Gone With the Wind* last night. Didn't want any interruptions, you know. Sorry about that. Can I get you a beer?"

"Um, sure."

I got two beers from the kitchen. Jude nodded at the TV screen. "So, did you just watch part of it last night? This is *Gone With the Wind* right now, isn't it? I know it's pretty long."

I searched for a light, cigarette in my mouth. Quest for fire. "Two hundred and thirty one minutes. Do you have a light? Oh, never mind, here it is. Actually, I watched it all last night. I'm watching it again now. I'll just turn it back on, if you don't mind...turn the sound down. I've seen it enough times that it doesn't matter if I miss a little. Especially this boring shit about the Civil War."

"How many times have you seen it?"

"Oh, man, I have no idea. This would be the third time this month, though."

"Kate, I think you need to get out more."

"Don't worry about me. I just love this movie, that's all. That Ashley Wilkes, he's the most maddening fictional character. But you know, I could turn this off. I will. How rude of me."

I woke up on the couch later that night. Jude was gone, probably back at her parents' house. Before she left she'd covered me with a blanket. She'd also straightened up, to my embarrassment. The note on the coffee table said she'd come by again tomorrow, maybe we could go out for lunch before she left for the airport. Under the note was an article I'd cut out of the newspaper and promptly lost a few days before. She would find it, librarian. It was a local-boy-makes-good piece about Dave Graham, Niall's brother, and a solo piano performance he recently gave at Carnegie Hall. I would have liked to have been there. And I would have been in the cheap seats, so he wouldn't have seen what a ratbag I looked like. Although he probably wouldn't have recognized me. Some days, I didn't even recognize me. Maybe it was better that way.

Seeing Jude, talking to her again had been great, though I was ashamed that she had to see how much my life had fallen to shit. Maybe I didn't even realize until then how much it had fallen to shit. I was just glad we hadn't got around to talking about my love life.

Clare and I had gone for a drink a couple of months after I kicked Gabe out. After a while one of the bartenders caught my eye. He had the slight stoop many tall men have, dirty blond hair cut short, an easy smile, wore a dark shirt buttoned almost up to the top. Just where he stood behind the bar, the downy hair on the nape of his neck was backlit and I couldn't stop looking at him. I had a sudden and powerful desire to taste his flesh.

"See that bartender?" I asked Clare.

She took one look at him. "You mean the one that looks like Niall Graham? The boy?" Shit. Was it that obvious?

She tried to convince me that picking up this young man ten or fifteen years my junior was a bad idea. Intellectually, I agreed. But he was there, in front of my eyes, noticing me noticing him. He proved to be incredibly easy to pick up. Funny, this sort of thing had seemed much more difficult years ago. I went over to the bar to pay for our drinks, gave him my credit card. He handed me the slip to sign.

"I want your autograph," he told me. "'Cause you look like a celebrity."

Now there's a line a guy over 21 wouldn't even think of using. He and I took a cab back to my place.

Rob was not a skilled lover, not a technically proficient lover. But he was eager and long-winded. And I could barely remember a man being grateful before, except for maybe Niall, at the beginning, before it got all miserable between us. He left before I woke the next morning, no note, no phone number, no last name, and I felt a little cheap, a little dirty. But it was probably better that way. Better that Clare think this was just a momentary indiscretion.

Which proved not to be the case. It was actually the start of a disturbing trend, one that carried on for months and threatened to resume at any time. There seemed to be a surfeit of young men around (I didn't have the heart to think of them as boys) who resembled Niall. Had there always been and I'd just failed to notice them before? Did the inevitable cycles of fashion give a vaguely retro, vaguely late-seventies look to young men? Whatever it was, they suddenly brought themselves to my attention. I couldn't resist picking them up in malls, in bookstores, in bars, and bringing them home. Some were strictly one-night affairs, others I might see a few times before calling it off. Finally, I resolved to stop altogether. It was too depressing, this ghoulish and futile attempt to relive the past. Not to mention risky. But then I came to see that I just did it to fill in the emptiness, so to speak. I was using desire to fend off something, I wasn't sure what. Loneliness, death maybe. I wanted to drive the sadness out, I wanted to have control of that part of my life again. Maybe it was something like what Maggie was doing, I realized. Worse was the realization that these encounters soon ceased to gratify me. Was it because there was no challenge in picking these guys up? It had mystified me at first that I could pick them up at all looking the way I did. Maybe I didn't really look as bad as I thought. Then I remembered that Marianne woman at The Calgarian so long ago. She wasn't attractive. But she was available, and experienced. Was I becoming like her? Thinking about that made celibacy sound downright appealing.

24. August 1995

Maggie called one night, said she'd be in town on the weekend and if I wanted to get together with her we could meet at The Unicorn at 2.00 on Saturday afternoon. I felt guilty about not talking to her much at my wedding. She had made the effort to come, after all, in spite of the blow-out we'd had that day in Seattle, which I also still felt guilty about. Still, did you stay friends with someone because you felt guilty? And were we friends in any real sense anymore? Probably not, but we'd known each other so long, and for much of that time, so well, that I imagined we'd know each other as long as we lived. And I didn't want there to be this chasm between us anymore. So I waited for her at The Unicorn once again, the dark basement bar seeming even darker and cooler on a bright, hot afternoon. And Maggie, as always, was late. But knowing her as I did, I arrived 45 minutes late myself, so I only had to wait about ten minutes for Mystress Xquisite Payne, as she referred to herself professionally, to arrive.

And arrive she did. Every man in the place stared at her, and most of the women, too. Regal, imperious, she swept into the bar in a long black leather cape that covered everything from her long white neck to the top of her thigh-high black four-inch heeled boots. Her long, teased hair was flame red, and under the cape she wore black leather pants and a tailored white silk blouse.

"You look casual today," I remarked.

"Well, you know, I'm on holidays." Her Polish accent was back these days. She'd worked hard at getting rid of it when we were kids and you could just barely detect it by the time we were in high school. Now it was part of the act: exotic, mysterious.

She mentioned when she called that she and a pal, who called herself Mistress Domina, had a discreet little chamber set up in an innocuous-looking house and apparently made a fortune. But it sounded like there might be some tension between the business partners.

"That fucking bitch!" Maggie growled, when I asked about Mistress Domina (or Donna, as she used to be known). "I could kill her! I never want to talk about her again!"

"Okay, but before you stop talking about her, tell me what happened."

"Does *Bondage Yoga* mean anything to you?"

"Of course I've heard of it." Who hadn't? *Bondage Yoga* was only the top selling exercise/spirituality/alternative sexuality video in North America just then. "What does that have to do with anything?"

"It was *my* idea! Like a fool, I told her about it and she just laughed at me, called it ridiculous. Next thing I know, she tells me she's had it with the BDSM line, sells me her half of the business and moves to California. And a few months later, wham! *Bondage Yoga* is everywhere! She got that thing produced in a hurry. Who knew the mainstream would take to it so well? I can't believe Mistress Domina could be so cruel to me, her one true friend!"

She was close to tears. "Maggie, I hate to see you like this. What can I get you to drink?"

"Drink? My body is a temple. Would I defile such a treasure with poison?"

I sighed. "Well, I sure could use a drink, Mag. Would you like a club soda?"

"All right."

When I returned from the bar I found her composed and calm again, to my relief. "Enough about Mistress Domina. On to more interesting conversation. I've been thinking lately, it's kind of funny how we got to be in the same business, you and me," she said.

"I guess we are. I never thought about it that way. Of course, you're actually *doing* these things, so that makes it a little different."

She arched one of her carefully shaped eyebrows. "You don't mean to tell me that you're not?"

"Well, no. And actually, I'm pretty much celibate at the moment. Do you want to know something else? I'm fed up with writing erotica. I've got a head full of ideas, stacks and stacks of serious writing, real writing that I keep sending out over and over again, and I just keep getting it back. I keep writing the erotica because it keeps selling, but sometimes I wish I'd never started. And in case you're wondering, most of the stuff I've written about, I've never done at all."

"You're joking. It's convincing, you know."

"Gee, thanks. I'll take a compliment whenever I can get it. But coming from an expert like you, it really means something."

"But what's all this about celibacy? How awful. Don't worry, though. I'm sure once you lose a few pounds, that will all change."

Ah, Maggie was cruel even when you weren't paying for it. I'd been waiting for her to make some crack about the weight I'd put on. I wish I could report that I'm one of those nervous types that loses ten pounds under stress, but I'm afraid it's quite the opposite. "There just isn't anybody right now. It's okay. When it happens, it'll happen." I declined to mention my little string of lovers, or sexual partners, more accurately. The shame was too much.

We talked about my trip to Seattle, years before. "I'm sorry I was so nasty," I said. "I guess I was just shocked by what you told me."

"That's all right. I forgive you."

"Don't take this the wrong way or anything, but I hope you'll find peace someday. You know, that you'll be able to be just Maggie again."

"Actually, I'm very close to finding peace. You'd be surprised."

"I'm glad to hear that." Maybe she'd gone to get some help after all, I thought.

We talked for another hour or so, mostly about the strange desires of her clientele, and then we decided to hit the road. Or I guess we did; that part is fuzzy. I know we left, anyway, made our way over to the hot rented red Lexus she'd parked a block or so away. I banged my head as I got in while she started it up.

"Kate, you are very drunk. Lucky for you, I'm driving," she said, as she shook her head and passed me a joint. "Want a hit?" The tires squealed on the loose gravel, we pulled out of the parking-lot and hit the road. In a big way.

"I don't know if we should do this when we're driving. Anyway, I thought you said your body was a temple," I said, and took a long puff, released it slowly. "Hey, what is *in* this?"

"Cocaine, dear. And a little tobacco to make it burn. But it's pure organic tobacco that a client of mine grows privately. You didn't think I'd pollute myself with that stinking pot you're so fond of, did you?"

"I suppose you think cocaine is some kind of health food. I don't want any more of that stuff. It weirds me out. Watch it!" I screamed as Maggie changed lanes without looking, almost plowed into a van. She drove like a maniac at the best of times. Today she didn't seem to notice or care that this was rush hour traffic downtown. She was completely oblivious to the world around her, just like she'd always been but more so. She wove in and out of traffic at top speed, took insane chances. My heart lodged in my throat.

"Maggie, I don't think you should be driving," I told her in a hoarse whisper.

"Don't worry about my driving. Anyway, soon it won't matter anymore." We sped east on Fifth Avenue, passed the Bow Valley Inn, the YWCA, stopped at the lights behind the Cecil Hotel. When they changed, the Langevin Bridge would take us over the Bow River and onto Edmonton Trail, back to my place.

"What do you mean?"

"I have tried to keep a good attitude over the years, in spite of all that's happened. But lately I've come to the conclusion that the world sucks, Kate. I know you think so. Look what it's done to you, poor thing. And look what it's done to me, and my sister. You can't trust anybody. Your family, your so-called friends and business partners. Even some of your own slaves turn out to be rotten. So I'm doing us both a favour. I'm going to gun it and go flying through the guard rail as soon as we get over the river."

"NO! We'll die! You can't—"

I stopped screaming in mid-sentence. The blood pounded in my ears, blocked out all other sound, and fear paralyzed my throat, like in those dreams I always had. Sweat prickled in my armpits, ran from my forehead and the nape of my neck. I dug my fingernails into the black leather seat, tried to find something to hold on to, as Maggie floored it and steered hard to the left. Suddenly we seemed to move in slow motion, and the car ripped surprisingly easily through the guardrail with a sickening grinding of metal against metal. Then we were airborne, sailing like a hang-glider over the Bow River.

In a strange moment of calm, fear left me. I realized I'd been over this bridge maybe a thousand times before, but never noticed the view until now, late afternoon sun sparkling on the surface of the green river. I also realized that this was big. This would be in the papers the next morning and on TV that very night. A-Channel was probably somewhere down there with a camera already. No doubt they'd interview the group of homeless men who enjoyed the weather on the grassy south side of the river, oblivious to the strange sight above them. Then the solid ground of the north riverbank rushed up toward the car and fear gripped my drunken heart once more. Oh, to able to speak, to be able to articulate the terror, the now almost certain knowledge that the last taste ever tasted in my mouth would be beer. Only it wasn't the taste of National Hotel draft, that sweet taste I'd never know again on this earth.

25. August 1995

Maggie's funeral took place on a serene afternoon a week after the accident. The driver's side of the car made impact with the smooth, round Bow River rocks on the north bank. The coroner said her neck snapped instantly. Apparently, it was lucky I'd been as drunk as I was. They told me all the alcohol I'd consumed had kept my body relaxed. Without it, I too might be dead, or seriously injured. This is my big chance to do a self-help piece, I thought: *How Drinking Saved My Life.* I got away with a concussion and a scar which ran from the outer corner of my left eye to the top of my head. When I could get up and move around in the hospital, on the second day I think, I looked at myself in the washroom mirror. A few bruises, both eyes ringed with black. A shaved spot on my head. I touched the scar, and was suddenly, strongly and strangely reminded of the last time I'd seen Niall. He'd touched me in the same place, looking at my hair. Must be the drugs, I thought, as I shook my injured head.

I felt awful, terrible about Maggie. What a waste, what a horrible waste of a life. But I sensed the release my old friend must have felt as we sailed off the bridge: free at last. Still, I couldn't help being angry with her for committing suicide. Oh yeah, and for trying to kill me, too. Where did she get off trying to kill me? But that was so like her the last few years. She always had her mind made up about what people thought and felt (she could read minds, after all), whatever they might say or do to the contrary.

The funeral wasn't at all what she would have wanted. She'd have wanted some kind of New Age affair with a drum chant to the Goddess and sweetgrass smudgepots and readings from the Tibetan Book of the Dead and all that. What else would do for the rightful creator of *Bondage Yoga*? But since she couldn't make her wishes known from the other side she got the standard Catholic funeral mass, followed by a graveside ceremony for the family. Which she would have just hated. She would have been spinning in her grave if she'd been in it yet. The only thing she would have liked was the warm, sunny afternoon. The scents of flowers and incense hung heavy inside the church. The last time I'd been in a church was for Carmen's funeral, not all that long before. Funny, you don't go to church for years and then people start to die on you. And I'd almost had a funeral of my own.

Jude and I sat a few pews behind the Iwaniszyn family. This was their second daughter's funeral, first Katya, now Maggie. I turned to see who was among the mourners and spotted Derek, Maggie's old flame, in the back. He looked tired, hot and uncomfortable in his suit.

"Are you all right?" Jude whispered. She couldn't believe they released me from the hospital after just three days. She only came to the funeral because she didn't think I should go alone, felt it might be too much for me. "I'm coming just to keep an eye on you, not as a mourner," she insisted. I assured her that I looked worse than I felt. If not for the bandage and the black eyes, nobody would have even noticed me. Besides, they gave me some happening painkillers in the little take-out bag from the hospital.

"I'm fine, don't worry. Look, Derek's here."

Jude turned and pretended to look in another direction while she regarded Derek out of the corner of her eye. "He shouldn't be here, either."

"Why not? He loved her."

"You two were the only ones crazy enough to love her."

"Shh...what a way to talk. I hope you're nicer to me at my funeral."

After the mass ended there was a reception in the church hall and Derek made his way over to me. He gave me a hug.

"How are you?" he asked.

"I'm all right. I'm here, aren't I? How are you? I haven't seen you in ages."

"I'm fine. Married, got two kids. Boys, one and three. The welding business is going well. Things are great."

"I'm glad to hear it. And I'm glad you made it here. Maggie would be happy to know you came."

Derek shook his still-gorgeous head. "I don't know about

that. She'd been hostile toward me the last few years. But I had to come. I've been in shock ever since I heard about it on the news. I can't believe how much this shook me up."

I had to smile. "Tell me about it."

"Listen, Kate, I've got to know. What happened?"

"What happened that day? Or what happened in general? Because this wasn't a freak accident or a random thing, or a whim. Not if you ask me." Derek's gaze was directed behind me now. I looked over my shoulder at Maggie's mother.

"Mrs. Iwaniszyn." I didn't know what to say. Maggie's mother put her long, bony arms around me for a moment, then pulled back, dabbed her eyes with an already wet, twisted tissue. Her black dress made her sharp features look even more severe, accentuated the hollows under her eyes.

"Kate," she said softly, as she fought back tears. "Thanks God you survived, dear. I'm so glad you could come today. And you, too, Derek. Seeing you here would have meant a lot to Magda. But don't let me interrupt. Go on."

I looked at Derek. I wouldn't be able to speak freely in front of Jadwiga Iwaniszyn. Or would I? Past Derek, at the far end of the room, I saw Maggie's father at the buffet table that the Catholic Women's League set up, popping those little crustless sandwiches into his fat mouth, looking like he hadn't a care in the world. If you didn't know him, you'd have never pegged him as one of the bereaved, much less the father. My hatred for him boiled up anew.

"Kate?" Maggie's mother snapped me out of it. "You were telling Derek what happened that day. I'm sorry to be an eavesdropper, but I have to know, too. What happened? They told us Magdalena drove the car off the bridge on purpose, but I can't believe it."

I looked hard at her for a second. I was sure she didn't believe it, sure she'd gone around for years not believing whatever she didn't want to deal with. She taught Maggie everything she knew about denial, no question about that. "She did drive off the bridge on purpose. She said our lives were messes and she was going to do us a favour and drive off it."

Mrs. Iwaniszyn's mouth pursed. Clearly, this wasn't the

answer she wanted to hear. "She must have been drunk."

"She wasn't. She'd had nothing to drink that afternoon. She'd smoked a little cocaine, but that had nothing to do with it. She was determined to kill herself. And she almost killed me, too."

Mrs. Iwaniszyn struggled with my words. "Why would Magda kill herself?"

Should I say it? Could the old bird stand it? A little way away, I spotted one of Maggie's cousins. She reminded me of Katya. "Mrs. Iwaniszyn, I think you should ask your husband that question."

Her eyes widened, her nostrils flared. I could see her jaw set, the muscles clench. "My husband never touched those girls in his life," she huffed.

Aha. She knew, she'd always known. She'd known and done nothing, pretended she had no idea. I boiled with rage inside, but tried to think, to plan what to say, to resist the urge to put my hands around her skinny neck and throttle her.

"I didn't *say* anything like that," I said after a moment. "I only said you should ask him why your daughter killed herself."

She burst into tears and rushed off into the arms of her family, who took her outside for some fresh air. Artur tried to comfort her as they climbed the stairs, but she beat him away with her purse. He stood stunned at the bottom of the stairs, watched his wife being taken out the door. He looked over at me and I gave him a smile and wave. He ran his hand nervously through his hair and rushed out to his wife.

I felt a twinge of guilt. Once a Catholic, always a Catholic. "I shouldn't have said it."

"Bullshit," said Derek. "Someone should have said that to her fifteen years ago, for all the good it would have done."

"I guess I should leave, now. Want to join us for a drink, Derek? Maybe we could talk some more."

"Sure. Let's get out of here."

We went to a nearby pub. Derek had a pint, looked like he could use one, and Jude joined him. I ordered a tea: I still felt damaged, frail. Well, that and I was on painkillers. The three of us were surprisingly lighthearted, considering we'd just been at a funeral. We talked about the old days. Eventually, I had to ask Derek if he'd heard from Niall lately.

"Yeah, I called him after I heard about the accident. Thought I should let him know. It shook him up quite a bit, I think. He's doing well. He's an ad copywriter with a big firm in Toronto. He works all the time from what I understand."

"Good for him," I answered. I found I couldn't bear to ask him anything else, now wished I hadn't mentioned Niall at all. I didn't expect to feel like that. Did Derek interpret this as coldness, indifference? Even though we hadn't seen each other in years, I think he knew me too well to think this. But I suddenly didn't want to know any more.

"Does it sound ridiculous to say that I feel like I've been given a second chance, here?" I asked. "I mean, I don't want to sound flaky...."

"Not at all," said Derek. "If you view things like this as opportunities, how much better is that than letting your world fall to shit around your feet?"

"Which would also be totally easy to do," added Jude.

I looked at each of them in turn. Two of the gentlest, kindest souls I've had the privilege to know. Was it the painkillers? Or the tea? I looked at Derek and Jude and knew they understood.

"It's just, I got so close to not being here anymore. Well, how can you squander something like that?"

"You can't," Derek said. "We have so little time, any of us, really."

I felt tired then and Jude took me home as it started to get dark. We were quiet in the car, didn't say much. I felt bad, wondered if I couldn't have done more to help Maggie over the years, been a better friend. But maybe the hurt was too bad, the damage too deep. Maybe there never would have been a way for her to heal. The worst part was I'd never know now one way or the other.

26. August 2006

The day of Jude's wedding was gorgeous, if a little hot. No wind, no clouds. She and Lisa stood on the dry yellow grass on the bank of the Bow River near Fort Calgary with a relaxed-looking Justice of the Peace and said their vows with a select few of us in attendance, just a stone's throw away from The National Hotel. Which almost became The National Condos. Imagine paying over $300,000 for a room at The National. But the developer's deal fell through, and now The National stands empty, boarded up to keep the crackheads out. Anyway. They both wore print sundresses and straw hats covered with flowers. I got to be one of the witnesses at the signing. They did their pictures right on the riverbank. On the way to the reception at Hillhurst-Sunnyside we all had a glass of champagne in the limo they'd rented. Lisa was a painter, a short, blond girl Jude had met two years before at a gallery opening. I liked Lisa a lot and was very happy for them.

Weddings are always a blast. Seemed like there were a lot of them in the late eighties, early nineties, then things slowed down. There's been the odd second wedding since then, but not even too many of them. And going to a wedding for a change is nice—the only time this crowd seems to get together now is for funerals. So Jude's wedding was the first I'd been to in a long time, and I was enjoying myself. I got a new vintage dress on eBay just for the occasion, a green chiffon fifties thing, not too poufy, and it fit like it was made for me. I was glad the dress worked out, because I felt nervous as hell when we got into the hall, like I knew I would.

"Remind me again why I'm doing this, Clare," I demanded, as we set up our equipment on the stage. We'd been coerced into providing some entertainment. We'd tried to get the rest of Misclairol back together for the event but it was just too hard to co-ordinate, so I was singing and she was playing guitar and singing backup.

"You're doing it as a personal favour to Jude. Also because I know that in your heart, you've wanted to do this again for years. It's not such a big deal. We're only doing a twenty-minute set and you're just singing this time. It'll fly by."

"I haven't done this in over twenty years, you know."

"You keep saying that. But you sounded great in rehearsals, so just forget it. Anyway, it's like riding a bicycle."

"I'm lousy at riding bicycles, too, remember? I used to have dreams about this all the time, about playing again. Only I haven't touched a guitar in fifteen years, and I don't know what songs we're doing, and we're going on in like two minutes."

"You need to relax. I think you're starting to hyperventilate. Let's go get a drink before we start."

When the time came and we climbed onto the stage again, my hands turned to ice. *This won't work. I can't sing. I'll fucking faint.* I picked up the cordless mike (never had these when I was young), turned it on, and waited for Clare to start the twelve-bar intro. I was sure that when I opened my mouth no sound would come out, just like in my dreams. But I relaxed as much as I could, listened to Clare. She sounded very funky, like a nineteen-thirties Duane Allman. Django Allman, perhaps. "My man's got a heart like a rock that's in the sea..." I started.

Hey. This was working. Of course I knew it would. We sounded great, looked great. I started to relax, to enjoy myself, even, and wondered how I could have such powerful stage fright when I actually loved performing? Maybe the question was, how could I enjoy performing when I had such powerful stage fright? It didn't matter. Right then, it felt so good to be in front of an audience again. I'd had no idea how I missed that, had no idea that I even could miss it until that moment. Maybe not playing guitar made me realize it. I'm not much of a guitarist and I always worried about fucking up during performances before. But I'm not a bad singer. Maybe I've needed to sing again for a long time and didn't know it. And applause? I'd forgotten how I used to get off on that. Now I realized I wanted to keep doing this until I dropped dead.

Maybe I would. Because something occurred to me then, something about stage fright. There's an enormous amount of energy that goes with stage fright. Anxiety and nervousness can build and build in the weeks and days before the show until it's almost immobilizing. But there's a small window there, when you first get on the stage, if you can ride the fear out and get going, you can channel all that energy into passion for what you're doing, make it work for you. I wonder why I didn't figure that out before.

As well as *St. Louis Blues*, we did *Should I Stay or Should I Go*, two songs Clare wrote and *Many Rivers to Cross*, and then we were done. But we did get asked for an encore, so we did *Going to the Chapel* and dedicated it to Jude and Lisa.

Onstage, I'd spotted John Petersen from The Sisters of Mercy, and when we finished he came up and gave me a big hug, almost picked me right up off the floor. He looked so different. Balding, greying, chubby. I was never thin myself, but I was down a fair bit from my-all time high in the post-Gabe days, pretty much where I was in the old days. John looked like someone's dad. He probably was someone's dad, I realized. He still had mischief in his eyes, though. Or maybe it was still rye.

"You guys sounded great," he said.

"Thanks, John. It was fun, actually."

"Makes me think I ought to get back to some music myself."

"Maybe you should."

"I heard you got married."

"Yes, I did. But that's all over, now. And what about you? I heard you got married a couple of years ago."

"I did. We did. Cheryl's out in Manitoba visiting her mother right now."

"So you're here by yourself, then."

"No, I did bring someone. Here he comes," he said, and nodded toward the bar.

Niall headed for us. Niall. Absolutely the last person I had expected to see at Jude's wedding, or anywhere else for that matter.

I had not seen him since that night at The National 21

years earlier. He looked different, too. He was a little heavier, and somehow seemed to have more hair than he used to, not less like men our age often do. I guess he just needed a haircut. For a second, I felt an impulse to run away, to hide. So much time had passed. How could he look at me and see anything but how much older I was, how long it had been? Not to mention everything else. But it was too late. Before I knew it my arms wrapped around him, his arms closed around me. My cheek rested against his chest and I felt him kiss the top of my head.

It felt so good. Better than I remembered, even.

"Niall," I whispered.

We stood back from each other. "You look great," he said, looking me up and down like he'd done so many times before.

I smiled, not sure where to look. I could not tell him that that was so what I wanted to hear, even though it was. "Thanks. You look good, too." I always did like how he looked in a suit, although he didn't wear a tie. But it was a fairly casual wedding, after all.

"How are you?"

"I am…freaked right out. And you?"

"I'm fine. And I enjoyed hearing you and Clare again. It's just like old times."

Was it like old times? A little, I supposed. I'm fine, he said. Must be nice. Me, I couldn't even tell how I felt. It was like talking to a ghost, so much time had passed.

The canned music started up again, Elvis Costello doing *Radio, Radio.*

"Would you like to dance?" he asked.

"Love to." Was this really happening? What was in that champagne?

After a couple of songs, we decided to take our drinks and go outside. It was hot inside the hall like years ago, when it was packed with much younger bodies gyrating to punk rock. Besides, it was too noisy to talk inside, like it used to be. Honestly, the more things change. I was sure we'd even leaned up against this same big old elm tree on the other side of the athletic field, drinks in hand, before.

"All right," I said. "What are you doing here?"

"My mom's health isn't so great, it's up and down. And she's on her own now, none of us are even in town anymore. So I've moved back in with her for a while. I just got here last week and John told me he was going to this wedding. So here I am. Surprised?"

"Oh, yeah, I'm surprised. Nice of you to move in with your mom." I tried to imagine moving in with Carmen. Nope.

He shrugged. "I guess. We'll see what happens. So tell me how you've been all this time."

"I'm afraid it's not all that interesting. I was married for a few years. We split up over ten years ago. My husband was an English prof at U of C with a special interest in female students."

"I think Frank Zappa said, 'If you want to get laid, go to college. If you want an education, go to the library'."

I had to smile. "Frank gets it right again. I have a part-time reference job at the Mount Royal College library, actually. Jude's a librarian and she got me the job. And I write some fiction. I used to make a little money writing erotica, but I lost interest."

"Erotica? Cool. Could I read some sometime?"

"I don't know about that. Maybe. Anyway, now I concentrate on the stuff I want to write. I heard you write, too. Copywriting."

The sun started to set. Maybe it would start to cool off now. He leaned forward and rested his elbows on his knees, and the hair on the back of his neck curled from the heat. I looked away and sipped my wine.

"Yeah, I did copywriting," he said. "But after a few years, I got sick of it. I know what you mean about losing interest. I've done a lot of things since then. Some writing, some music. I've had day jobs, too, of course. Waited tables, delivered mail for a while."

"Huh. Really. All these years I figured you were probably married off, house full of kids, giant mortgage. Living the dream, you know."

"Well, I never did go to law school."

"Probably just as well. It's funny you'd show up back here

now, because I'm about to move."

"No kidding. Where?"

"Victoria. I've finally had it with this place. Except for when I was in Tuktoyaktuk, I've been in Calgary all my life. And not that I've travelled a lot, but before whenever I went somewhere, I'd miss Calgary. I used to like living here. Sure, there were rednecks around, lots of old-money Conservatives. Sure, we've had one-party rule since 1971. I used to be able to ignore all that, and I used to defend Calgary when people would put it down. But a few years ago, I don't know if it's the city or me or what, I realized I couldn't stand it anymore."

"Is it the traffic?"

"It's a lot of things. The traffic's horrible. And I hate driving at the best of times. And then there's the boomtown attitude. It's all about money. It's about driving your SUV for an hour from your half-million dollar 5000-square foot house in the suburbs to pay $25 to park downtown every day. People are stressed, rushed, grim. The place is like Toronto but without the arts scene. So why would an old lefty punk rocker stay here?"

"Good question. I've been away for a long time, but it does seem different. Not in a good way. I think it is all about money for a lot of people."

"And the older I get the less money matters to me. Now I want to live somewhere where you don't have to deal with traffic gridlock and homicidal drivers all the time. Somewhere where they don't blow up hospitals, where they change the governing party once in a while. And I've always wanted to live by the ocean."

"I hear you. So when are you going?"

"Pretty soon, maybe in a month or so. I'm getting rid of stuff, scoping out places to live on the Internet, looking for a job out there. Another library job would be nice, but I guess I could do retail again for a while if I had to."

Eventually, we went back inside. For one thing, our drinks were empty. Besides, we were supposed to be there for Jude and Lisa. They did the wedding thing where they tried to visit with everyone, though, which left them unable to talk to anybody too long. And then they left earlyish, eager to begin that Vancouver Island honeymoon of theirs, no doubt. Seemed like everybody wanted to get out to the Island. I tried not to think about how a lot of people retire out there.

The party continued, but not for as long or as loud as you might expect. John was giving Niall a ride home, so I sleazed one off him, too. We pulled up in front of my building.

"Well, hey, thanks, John. Good to see you again. Hope you and Cheryl start up that family soon."

"Will do. You take care of yourself, Kate."

Niall got out of the car and walked me up to the door.

"Can we get together sometime soon?" he asked.

I smiled at him. I wondered what he would do if I said no. "Sure. Give me a call." I wrote my number on a page of the handy little pad in my purse that writers are always supposed to carry around with them. "Your mom still has the same phone number? 240-6013?"

"I can't believe you remembered that."

"I remember a lot of things. You may want to think twice before you call."

He pulled me close and we kissed, a real kiss this time, not on the head or the cheek like the last few times. And God, it was good. I could have stood there all night. John honked after a bit and I felt like I was seventeen again. Only I hoped I wasn't as stupid as I was then.

"I better go. It was great to see you again. I'll talk to you soon."

"Goodnight, Niall."

I got ready for bed, and squinted into the mirror in the bathroom as I brushed my teeth. I was not dreaming, I was not drunk. Well, not very drunk. But I still couldn't believe it. And although I was tired, I was still wound up. I got into bed but didn't fall asleep for a long time, and everything from the ceremony to sitting under the elm tree at the hall ran through my head, over and over. I wasn't convinced that it had all really happened.

He called me later the next day, just as I started to think he wouldn't. After all, I knew him rather well once. We decided to meet for dinner the next evening at Chianti's on 17th Avenue, just a few blocks from my apartment building. I hadn't been to Chianti's since Gabe and I lived in Sunalta.

After a while I worried that it might be bad juju to go to a place where Gabe and I had eaten so often. I almost called him back so we could pick somewhere else. Once I decided that was ridiculous, I started to worry about what to wear. After all, what kind of message did I want to send out? I wanted to look good, for sure. Did I want to look sexy? Maybe in an understated way. Looking too sexy would say, "desperate divorcée." I didn't want that, though God knows it was true. On the other hand, not looking sexy might say, "uninterested" or "dumpy." It was hard to know what to wear, and I changed my mind over and over. Finally I decided on jeans and a black T-shirt, and some nice Pedro Miralles black pointed-toe boots.

Then I walked over to the restaurant. We had arranged to meet at seven, and although Chianti's was only about a five-minute walk from my house I left at twenty-five to. Maybe this was a carry-over from driving. Maybe I expected pedestrian gridlock, two or three light waits to cross the streets. The thing was, I had been ready to go at six and I was so tired, tired of waiting. So of course I got there early. Since the weather was warm I picked a table out on the patio. Seventeenth Avenue is a busy street, maybe not the best place for a patio, but it was cooler outside than in the restaurant so that clinched it.

So now I sat on the patio looking far too eager, waited for Niall to show up. He'd probably be late. He'd probably stand me up. The waitress would come by and ask if I wanted to order and I'd say, "I'll wait until my friend gets here," only I'd trip over the word 'friend', I'd stutter, and she'd smirk and walk away. But then I saw him, actually, as he waited for the light to change across the street. He was early, too. He saw me and came and joined me. He also wore jeans and a T-shirt, although his boots were flats. I stood and we embraced again. Goddam, that felt good.

At the wedding, there had been a limit to how much we could really talk together, so over dinner we got caught up, or tried to. He got to hear all the sordid details of my life since we'd last seen each other and I heard all about his copywriting career and why he left it, the succession of jobs he'd had since then, and the succession of lovers he'd had. Funny, while he told me about some of the women in his life I felt a little flame of jealousy inside. How stupid, I thought, how childish. What did I expect, anyway? I told him about John and James. And Jude, and Gabe. Well, I didn't mention anything about those young men a few years ago. None of his business, right? Still, I hadn't expected to feel jealous. I didn't want to hear anymore about these women. Just when I thought I would scream, the waitress cleared our table and emptied the last of the wine into our glasses, and that seemed to put an end to that thread of conversation, mercifully.

"Things seem to be going well for you, now," he said.

"If you'd seen me a few years ago, you wouldn't have said so. I don't know. If there's one thing I've finally figured out it's this: you'd better deal with the shit in your life before it deals with you. Look at my mom, look at Maggie. They just let it pile up until it killed them both, one way or another. And I don't want to die for a long time yet. My life was on the skids before the accident. My marriage fell apart, my mother's death really messed me up. Brought up a lot of issues that I didn't want to face. So I drank a lot, didn't care what happened to me. Actually, in a way Maggie did me a favour by trying to kill me."

"How can you say that?"

"Well, it certainly helped change my life."

"Almost ended it, too."

"Yeah. Sometimes that's just what has to happen, though."

"I guess. I think some coffee and liqueurs should happen right about now, don't you?"

"Sure."

Part way through dinner he had stretched his long legs out under the table around either side of me, so that they almost touched my legs. It felt possessive to me and for a while I couldn't decide whether or not I resented it. After all, did he think he could just drop into my life after 21 years and pick up right where we left off? That would not, could not happen again, at least not the way it was. I hoped he understood that. More, I hoped *I* understood that. Still, I felt like I'd lived three lives, at least, since the old days. I just wasn't sure about any of this at all. After a while, he rested one leg up against mine, and every time he moved a little I had to take a deep breath. It felt so good, and yet. And yet. Part of me, and not a small part, said *wait a minute.* Not that I didn't want this. I did. I just didn't want it to be bad, like it was before. But until things got going, how would I know whether they were bad or not? I guessed I would have to take a chance. I guessed I would have to trust myself not to let him treat me like he did before.

That was the scary part. Could I do it?

I find the trouble with liqueurs is they tend to break down my resolve when it comes to dessert. Dessert and stuff like that. Before I knew it my Sambuca and coffee was gone and we waited for the waitress to come back with Niall's credit card. He had slipped his hand over mine.

"So," he said. "What should we do now? Any ideas?"

I swallowed. Well, what the hell would I say, eh? I thought about telling him I wanted to turn in early. I thought about saying a lot of things. What I did finally say was, I'm afraid, very predictable: I asked him if he'd like to come see my place.

"It's small, though, and kind of hot," I warned him.

"I'm sure we'll find a way to deal with it."

What Niall didn't know was that I had it all figured out this time. I'm not a pushover, you know, I would tell him. Yes, I would tell him that very soon. I showed him around my warm little apartment, not that there was much to show, and picked out some music while he opened the bottle of wine he'd brought. He poured us a couple of glasses and joined me in the living-room. I stood and looked out the window at the street below, watching a couple walk by with their dog while I decided how exactly I would tell him things were different. Then in a rare moment of lucidity I realized it would be best just to show him things were different, instead of telling him.

"Here you go," he said, passing me a glass.

"Thanks, Niall."

"How about a toast?"

"Sure. What are we toasting?"

"To old friends, how about that?"

"To old friends it is."

We both had a sip and put our glasses on the windowsill. He slid his hands over my hips and pulled me close to him. And, oh God, the things running through my mind as we looked into each other's eyes. How I wanted him at that moment, and yet how I didn't want to feel like I used to. Would one night with him start that all again? And if it did, maybe we were both different. Or maybe we weren't. It was so hard to know. And even after all the time we'd been apart, or maybe because of it, I wanted to have him right then. I had to. He kissed me gently, once.

"How do you feel?" he asked, as he moved his hands up and down my back.

"Do you really want to know?'

"Of course I do. Do you want me to go first?"

"That's a good idea. Tell me how you feel."

"I feel fantastic. I feel like I want to make love to you all night."

Deep breath. "That's pretty much the way I feel, too. Except, you know, things are different now."

"You mean we're both older, we've had a lot of experiences...."

"And we're maybe a little wiser, a little more careful. Maybe we're a bit afraid, too."

"You don't have to be afraid of me. I won't hurt you."

"I guess I'll just have to trust you, Niall. There's no way you can leave here without coming to bed with me."

After that we didn't talk for quite a while. When I pulled myself against him I could feel he was already hard, and once that was established it seemed like we should get naked pretty fast. I had worried before about how being so much older would affect things. After all, the last time we'd had sex we were firm, young people in our early twenties who'd never even heard of gravity. But none of that seemed to matter at all. We were as hot for each other as we'd ever been, maybe hotter. It felt like we had to do it right then, right there, no time to go into the bedroom or even move very far. Before long he had me hoisted up onto the nearest piece of furniture, which happened to be the overstuffed thirties armchair I inherited. Overstuffed, indeed. We went at it with a fervour I only dimly recalled from my long ago youth, and I had to bite my lip when I thought about my neighbours. Oh, God. People my age could go into cardiac arrest from something like this, couldn't they?

It took me a minute to catch my breath, splayed all over my good chair with him inside me. "Holy shit, buddy. Fastest gun in the west or what?"

"Yeah. And I'm not even a westerner anymore."

"You eastern bums and creeps are all the same."

He smiled, and got up. "Nice chair," he said.

"It was my grandmother's," I said.

"Think it's ever been used for that before?"

"I'd prefer not to think about that, thanks. How about bringing our drinks over here?"

"I have a better idea. Why don't I just take them into the bedroom? I'll bring the bottle, too."

Okay, so far things weren't really that different than they used to be, not yet. But I would show him soon. Really.

27. September 2006

I wake up and for a second am confused to find my legs tangled up in something. Other legs, Niall's legs, I remember. Of course. I roll over and he's still fast asleep, snoring in fact. Did he used to snore? I suppose so. I can't remember, actually. I let him sleep and gently pull myself a little closer to him, lean my cheek against his back, feel his breath rise and fall. His snores, I mean.

This feels so good. Better than it used to, I think, and I don't understand why. Oh, well. Why analyze it? Why not just enjoy?

152

Last night was so good. Again. He came over for dinner. I made clam linguine, an old never-fail standby of mine. Outside it poured, and we lit candles and sat on the couch and drank wine and talked after dinner. We talked for hours. We are both phenomenal talkers, something else I'd forgotten about. We listened to music too, of course. And then we ended up here. Maybe it was the Chopin. Chopin always gets me. God, what is it? Even sex seems better than it used to. Maybe because it doesn't matter to me the way it used to. Maybe it's just that we're so, er, experienced now.

Eventually I have to get up. I have to piss like a racehorse, and I really need a coffee. Some food would be good, too.

I'm in the kitchen in my striped pyjamas, waiting for the coffee to brew, and I rustle around in the fridge for something to eat. There isn't much. Pickles, peanut butter, some eggs of a certain age. I hope Niall's not too hungry. I hear him come up behind me and he puts his warm hands on my hips. I straighten and he nuzzles the back of my neck, his whiskers scratch a little.

"Good morning," he whispers. His soft breath in my ear still makes me shudder. He turns me around to face him and kisses me.

"Morning. How are you?"

"Very well. I need a coffee, though."

"It's coming. Hang on."

"What's that song you've been humming?"

"It's called *Victoria*."

"That old Kinks song?"

"Yeah. It runs through my head a lot. For obvious reasons. Actually, The Kinks and the West Coast have been entwined in my mind since Clare and I went out to Vancouver to see them."

"That was a long time ago."

"Yeah, 1981. Every time I go out to the coast I think of that concert. And I think of how the next night at their show in Edmonton, Jude pulled the piece of masking tape that said 'Edmonton' off the stage in front of the one of the floor mics before the show. I guess it was pretty funny when Ray Davies was about to launch into his 'Hello, name-of-city-here' thing and he had no idea where he was."

"I wish I'd seen that. So, I guess you've got Victoria on your mind, then. Does this mean you're still thinking of moving?"

"Well, yes. I am moving, I'm not just thinking of it. I'm staying with a friend while I look for a job and an apartment, have a little money saved. I'm ready."

I get up and pour us a coffee and we go sit on the couch again. The light from outside is grey, soft. It's not raining at the moment but it looks like it could start anytime. I move our glasses from last night and the stack of CD cases on the coffee table. He is quiet. He has picked up the Horowitz Chopin CD case and studies it carefully. I know he's really not that interested in Old Vladimir.

"Are you hungry?" I ask.

"Not really. Not yet." He doesn't look at me, still checks out Vladimir. Is he sulky? This is not like him, not like the him I used to know, anyway.

"What's the matter, Niall?"

"I guess I'm just surprised you're leaving, that's all."

"Yeah, I can see that. I mean, I've been here forever. All the more reason to leave, if you ask me."

He's quiet again. I have to persist. "Did you think I might change my mind now that you're back?"

"I don't know. Maybe."

"Oh, Niall. You know what? I've wished so many times that you'd come back to me. I always thought I could make it work if I had another chance, that things would be different."

"They are different."

"Yes. They are. But they're not different enough. Do you know why? Because I really want to go. I feel like I belong there. I even know some people out there in a blues band that plays around, and I'm going to go jam with them, see what happens."

"You sounded great at the wedding."

"Thanks. And I realized how much I missed music, you know? Now I really want to spend some time doing this. This band's called Holy Mother. They play a lot of benefits and that kind of thing. They're doing one for a group that helps victims of sexual abuse at the end of October, a Hallowe'en party gig. I like the idea of doing stuff like that. So I had my mind made up, my plans all made. And then you show up out of nowhere after twenty one years just as I'm about to take the plunge and get out of this town."

"So you haven't even considered staying?"

"Of course I have. The first thing I thought when I saw you at Jude's wedding was how it figured you would come back to town just as I was about to leave. And every day since then it's been on my mind almost all the time. But the thing is, if I stayed here to be with you, I'd need a commitment."

He just looks at me. Exactly. A commitment, Niall Graham. From you, a guy who couldn't even commit to a pet goldfish.

"If you could do that, I'd stay. But I just can't put myself through all the insecurity and jealousy and misery again."

"Misery? Come on."

"Yes, misery. What do you think I felt all those times you ignored me for weeks at a time? I was miserable. Can you honestly say you won't do that to me again?"

"I don't know."

"Exactly. And I can't take that chance. I don't think I could stand a broken heart again, not at my advanced age."

He's finished his coffee now, leans back and rests against my shoulder. For a long time we don't say anything. I take sips of my coffee, rest my cheek on his head. Fuck, I am so damn conflicted right now. Why does this have to be so hard? If I had any notion it could really be like this forever, I would stay. I would do anything. My body and my heart scream out for me to do it—stay, are you crazy? But I know better. Maybe it would be like this for a while, one little room our everywhere. And then one night I'd be wondering where he was. Sooner or later he'd be gone for days at a time. Sooner or later I would feel like I did back in the old days. Sooner or later I would feel like shit.

"Let's go get something to eat," he finally says.

I have to see him just one more time before I go. Tomorrow morning I'm renting a van with the money I got when I sold my car, then I'll drive out to Victoria. I got rid of everything

I wanted to. I'm amazed at how I could always cut it down more. Just when I thought I'd got rid of everything I could, I'd find more stuff that I didn't really need. Like I kept some of my books. With most of them I thought, will I ever read this again? If I want to, can't I just get it from a library or buy another one? There's my stereo, my CDs, my computer. I had to keep those. Clothes, I cut to the minimum. I kept the current wear pile, some seasonal items, only my favourite vintage stuff, and the rest I gave away. Most of the furniture I got rid of except some of my grandmother's stuff, like the chair I've always loved. And now it's just acquired some new memories. Kept my TV because it would cost too much to buy a new one, and I need it to watch movies. If only I could live like this all the time, I think. My place would finally look like an IKEA flyer. But I know myself too well. I'm a packrat. And once I get into those thrift stores and garage sales in Victoria, it'll be back to the usual rotating junk collection that passes for decor around here. Oh well.

It's the middle of a warm Sunday afternoon and we meet on Prince's Island. I'm a little tired. I'd been out late the night before with Jude and Clare, said goodbye to them. Although the two of them are planning a joint Victoria trip already, so it's not goodbye forever, that's for sure. Maybe I shouldn't have agreed to see Niall again but I haven't any idea how not to, never did. Even so, it's different than it used to be. At last, I can be around him and think rationally. The Niall part of my brain finally did disappear, or at least diminish. When I tried to explain this to Clare and Jude they didn't believe me. Like a couple of disapproving parents, those two. I feel like I did when I sneaked out to the movies once with a boy in Grade 10, after Carmen told me I was not allowed to go out with boys until I was sixteen.

Niall and I discreetly smoke a fatty in the trees, wander around the park among the kids and dogs and young couples. After a while we walk in silence. Unusual for us, especially under the circumstances. Any other time I would have thought, that's okay, we're comfortable with each other. We don't have to talk all the time. But this time I know it's more of a case of the elephant in the room, the thing taking up all the space and crushing the little furniture I have left, but neither of us wants to talk about it. Finally he breaks the silence.

"So when are you getting up tomorrow?"

"I don't know. Not too early, I don't think. I don't have that much to do. I'm pretty much packed. I'll go and get the van after breakfast, load it up and that'll be it."

"You'll be okay driving there by yourself?"

"Sure. I mean, I don't like driving in general that much, but September's a great time of year for it. And I'm not going to barrel all the way through. I'll probably stop in Salmon Arm or Kamloops and do the rest the next day. There's no rush."

"What if something happens with the van?"

"I'll be fine. Don't worry. Want to come with me?"

"I can't."

"Why not? Your mom's okay right now, isn't she? You could come out and stay for a few weeks. You might get to like it."

"I just can't. You know I can't."

You bet I know, I think. I allow myself to smile, but bite my tongue. After all, what if you did get to like it, what then? It would just never do.

Some cloud starts to move in before long, the wind feels cooler now. This is September, don't forget. My feelings do a weird dance. Still, I'm doing the right thing. I am, I tell myself again. I want to move.

"Will you need some help loading up?" he asks.

"That would be great."

"So what time should I come by?"

"Well, if you come over now, you'll already be there in the morning, right?"

He smiles. That's good to see. He's been a little too serious this afternoon. "That's true."

"We could watch a movie. My DVD player's still set up."

"Okay. You have *Gone With the Wind*, don't you? I saw it once a long time ago, but I'd like to see it again."

"Sure. It's kind of long, but we have lots of time."

"Lots of time," he agrees. "Let's go, then."

As we walk over the bridge back to downtown, I feel a certain lightness I haven't felt in a long, long time and a smile keeps creeping over my face. It's not being stoned, it's not being amused, it's something else. I'm not really sure what.

Well. Why analyze it?

The next morning things go exactly as I'd planned. Even better, because I didn't expect to have Niall around to help me. We go get the van, come back and throw the few unpacked things into boxes, then we load the furniture and boxes. I vacuum, give the apartment a once over and drop my keys in the resident manager's mailbox. Now we stand on the sidewalk in front of my building beside the van. The ancient poplars on my street are losing their leaves already. In two weeks they'll be bare, and then it'll start to get cold. I so won't miss that. I won't miss that at all.

I throw my arms around him and hold him as tight as I can, try not to think about that time he left for Toronto all those years ago. But of course, that's all I can think of. My eyes sting a little, but I blink it back. "Thanks for all your help. It would have been a bit of a trick getting that chair into this thing by myself."

"You're welcome. Looks like you've got a beautiful day for it."

"Yeah, I think so. Sure you don't want to come with me, now?"

He puts a finger over my lips and shakes his head. Then we kiss and for just a moment, you know what I think. I think I can't leave him, I can't really.

"Call me when you get out there, okay?" He has slid his chin onto my shoulder as he asks me this so that I can't see his face. I feel a giant lump in my throat.

"I will. Don't worry," I whisper.

We stand like this for a long time, and finally we pull back to look at each other and kiss once more. "You'll have to come and see me once I get settled."

"Sure."

"Well, I should go. Goodbye, Niall."

"Goodbye, Kate. Don't forget to call."

"I won't."

I get in, put on my seatbelt, start the van up. I wave at him. We both smile and I cry a little, too, and wonder if he is. I decide I don't want to look hard enough to find out. This is very hard as it is. I pull away, and wave again. I watch him as long as I can in the rear-view mirror and he gets smaller and smaller. For just a minute I'm sure my heart will break and I almost turn around. Then I turn on to 17th Avenue and drive due west. Riding westward.

After a while I put the mixed tunes CD Clare burnt for me into the van's CD player. She's put some great stuff on it. The sixties bands I love, like The Electric Prunes doing *I Had Too Much to Dream Last Night*, The Beau Brummels doing *Laugh, Laugh*. Blues, like Elmore James' *Dust My Broom*, Howlin' Wolf doing *Killing Floor*. Even some newer stuff like *Date With the Night* by The Yeah Yeah Yeahs and *Hate to Say I Told You So* by The Hives. The music makes me feel a whole lot better.

One thing I do like about being on the road is that you can think, clear your head. I've been thinking: I've done some stupid things in my day, selfish things, nasty things, things I regret. But right now I'm okay with all that. Right now I feel so optimistic, like I've got my whole life ahead of me. It feels great. Yet I'm leaving so much behind. Man.

Somewhere around the Banff park gates I realize that same smile as yesterday has crept over my face. Only this time I know what it is—I'm happy. This is so what I want to do right now. And something occurs to me. I'm better now. I really am better. Weird, eh? And I'm sure I'll see Niall again, as sure as you can be about anything in this life. Or as sure as you can be about him, anyhow.

It is a nice day for driving, clear and warm, and when I finally get out of town the foothills roll out in front of me, yellow, brown and green. Beyond them the mountains are flat blue and white, look cold, far away. And I'll drive right through them, past them. Tomorrow night I'll be at the edge of the continent, the edge of the world.

LORI HAHNEL played with the Virgins in Calgary from 1979 to 1983. Her short fiction has been broadcast on CBC Radio and published in *The Fiddlehead*, *Prairie Fire* and *Room Magazine*. A collection of short fiction, *Nothing Sacred*, is forthcoming in 2009, and she is currently at work on a second novel. See www.lorihahnel.ca.

DISCARD